# Cyber. kdz :2

## A PICTURE'S WORTH

*Other Avon Camelot Books in the*
**Cyber.kdz** *Series*
*by Bruce Balan*

#1: In Search of Scum

Coming Soon

#3: The Great NASA Flu

The Cyber.kdz say they have created BRUCE BALAN to serve as a front for their book-writing operations. He is a computer-generated character—an artificial persona—designed to shield them from discovery and programmed to do exactly what he is told.

However, Bruce's publisher will tell you that he's published five books (including *The Cherry Migration* and *Pie in the Sky*), owned a software development company, worked an assortment of jobs (from veterinary assistant to programmer to sous-chef) and specializes in designing client/server database applications. They insist he lives with his wife, Dana, and their dog and cat in Northern California's Silicon Valley.

Only Dana, the dog, and the cat know who is telling the truth.

# Cyber.kdz :2

## A PICTURE'S WORTH

AN AVON CAMELOT BOOK

AVON BOOKS
A division of
The Hearst Corporation
1350 Avenue of the Americas
New York, New York 10019

Copyright © 1997 by Bruce Balan
Published by arrangement with the author
Visit our website at **http://AvonBooks.com**
Library of Congress Catalog Card Number: 96-94905
ISBN: 0-380-78515-3
RL: 4.9

First Avon Camelot Printing: April 1997

CAMELOT TRADEMARK REG. U.S. PAT. OFF. AND IN OTHER COUNTRIES, MARCA REGISTRADA, HECHO EN U.S.A.

Printed in the U.S.A.

OPM  10  9  8  7  6  5  4  3  2  1

For Sarah

# Acknowledgments

Thanks to Dana Balan, Patrick van Gool, Marion van Utteren, Marcia Renno-Light, April Halprin Wayland, Irving Cox, Joanne Rocklin, Julieann Steger, Andy Anderlini, Richard Clark, Marie Brindze, Vick Beyrouti, Kelly Quiroz, Neil Ross, DDS, Peggy Breyer, Andy Sinton, Eli Frankel, Jessica Bagdorf, Debbie Abilock and the students of the Nueva School Library Class, and my editor, Gwen Montgomery.

# [1]

The class burst into applause. Becky couldn't believe it. Was she dreaming? She knew her presentation was good, but she didn't think it was *that* good. Besides, no one at school had ever cheered for her before. It wasn't like she was popular or anything.

"Innnn . . . credible! Fantastic, Becky!" Mr. Optol, her history teacher, was clapping louder than anyone else. "Just fantastic! One of the best presentations I've ever had. Does anyone have any questions?"

Shareesh Agah raised his hand.

"How fast did you say those Byzantine telegraph messages went?" he asked.

"Pretty fast," Becky answered. "The system used light signals from torches and mirrors. There were guardposts on every hilltop between the capital and the frontier. A message sent from the Cilician border, six hundred miles away, was received in Byzantium in an hour."

"Wow," Shareesh said. "That's faster than most planes!"

"Yeah," Becky continued, "and that wasn't even the longest light telegraph. Around nine hundred A.D. there was a string of beacons along the coast of North Africa that was over two thousand miles long."

Becky's presentation had been on communication in the ancient world. Her classmates were impressed with the technology invented thousands of years ago. Mr. Optol was impressed with the quality of Becky's research. Becky took her seat smiling.

Mr. Optol leaned against his desk. "I hope those of you who haven't had your chance up here yet will use what you saw as an example of excellent research and a well-thought-out presentation." He smiled again at Becky. "Great job."

Mr. Optol turned toward his desk and grabbed a stack of papers. "Okay, let's move on. I've graded your essay tests."

A collective groan went up from the class.

Mr. Optol continued. "And I can't believe some of the scores!"

The students brightened as they heard the enthusiasm in his voice.

"They are absolutely . . . positively . . . incredibly . . . *awful!*"

The groan was even louder this time.

"C'mon! I can't take this anymore! I'm not standing up here for my health, you know. You're gonna kill me if you don't start listening! I've decided to retire at the end of the year if your test scores don't improve. *The grades better grow, or Mr. O's gonna go!*"

Darren Taylor raised his hand.

"Yes, Darren?"

"My sister was in your class last year and she said you made the same threat. Same poem, too."

The students snickered.

"She did, did she?" Mr. O said sarcastically. "Did her test scores improve?"

"Yeah, I think so . . ."

"Well, it worked, then, didn't it?"

Everyone laughed.

"All right, if my threatened retirement isn't enough, I'll have to think of something better." Mr. O stroked his clean-shaven chin. He was the youngest teacher at school and all the students loved him. They knew there was no way he was even close to retiring. "Okay, if everyone's scores don't improve by twenty percent, I'll fail the entire class. No exceptions!"

*"No!"* the class shouted.

"No?"

"Please don't, Mr. Optol!" Jenny Sloat was close to tears. "I can't fail! Like, my parents will just *kill* me. They said I can't try out for cheerleading next year if I, like, fail even *one* class! They're totally uncool . . . they just don't get it!"

"Ohhhh, noooo! That would be just, like, *awwwful,*" Darren teased.

The class burst out laughing.

"Calm down, everyone. I'll stick with my original threat. I think that will be enough. Because if I retire, at least half of you will be stuck with Mr. *Greemes* for sociology next year." Mr. Optol pronounced "Greemes" like *Greeeeeeemes* and said it through his nose. He rolled his eyes and dropped his lower lip. He continued in the silly voice, *"Hend I'm sshure hew whouldn't whant that, nohw, whould hew? Thihnk hof hall the whonderful fihlm strihps whe'd whatch. Whe'd hhhave so muhch fuhn..."*

The class laughed.

"Good. We've agreed, then. You study and I stay. *Show me what you know, you're gonna keep Mr. O.*"

While he talked, Mr. Optol walked down the aisles and

3

handed out the papers. Becky's high spirits had dulled somewhat. Mr. Optol had said all the scores were terrible. That had to include hers—and she'd been sure she'd aced this test.

Mr. O handed a paper to Jenny Sloat, who sat right in front of Becky. Becky could see the red F scribbled across the top. Jenny whimpered a little and reached into her pack for a tissue. Mr. Optol took a few more steps and dropped Becky's test in front of her.

He leaned over slightly and said quietly, "As usual, my perfect historian turns in a notable performance."

Becky looked down. The bright red A nearly jumped off the page.

Becky was glowing as she walked out of class. This was definitely the best day she'd had since she'd started at Bennington-Carver six and a half months ago. It had been a hard transition from middle school. Her best friend, Kim, who she'd gone to school with since they were eight, went to Chichester Prep. But Becky had received an academic scholarship to Bennington-Carver, a private school. Her parents could never have afforded it, and they were delighted. It seemed like a great opportunity, but Becky hated the fact that she'd had to face high school alone.

Most of the kids at Bennington-Carver lived in expensive apartments on Fifth Avenue or in the Village. Some were stuck-up, others just weren't that friendly. There had been plenty of jerks in middle school, but it didn't seem to matter as much when she was with Kim. It was worse now because she was by herself. It had been a tough year so far. But things were definitely looking up.

"Hey, fatso! Think you can move any slower . . . ?"

An arm shoved Becky aside. Her books thumped to the

floor. Three sophomores pushed past her and ran off down the hall.

Becky bit her tongue. "Just ignore them, Beck," she said to herself. "They're mindless barbarians. You know that. They make Attila look perfectly civilized." She collected her things and continued to her next class. She thought about Mr. O's praise. Remembering his warm smile as he'd applauded her presentation made her feel better.

It wasn't until she entered the locker room that it struck her where she was. She was feeling so good about history she had walked to seventh period without even thinking. How could she? It was the class she dreaded the most each day. P.E. was the worst.

Becky was overweight. That's what her mom said. But Becky (and plenty of the kids at school) called it *fat*. For years her parents had told her that her baby fat was just hanging on a little longer than her friends'. Her mom and dad didn't seem to mind, so neither did Becky. But the baby fat didn't go away as she got older. And over the last few years, as Kim started getting curves, Becky resigned herself to the fact that she would always look like this. So much so that she stopped noticing it. In the bathroom in the morning, she didn't really *see* who was standing behind the comb or toothbrush. She focused on the motion of the brush going back and forth and never looked at who was doing the brushing.

It wasn't like she didn't *care*. It wasn't important to her what people looked like. She liked people for who they were, not how they appeared. That's why she could start up conversations so easily with people on the subway or at the library. She cared about what people *thought*. What they did. What they wrote. It didn't matter how much you weighed if you were a great archaeologist. Who cared if you were heavy if you wrote *The History of the Roman Empire*? Fat didn't matter.

Except in P.E.

At first she was surprised and amazed that all these girls could be so cruel. The looks, the whispers, the jokes—she didn't understand why they tried so hard to make her feel bad. Why did they even care?

But for some reason that Becky didn't understand, they did. Fat mattered in high school.

"Roman emperors were often overweight," her father'd told her, trying to cheer her up months before, after her first miserable day in high school P.E. "And, you know, the bigger a Hawaiian queen was, the better."

"But that doesn't make anybody *like* me," Becky replied.

"It's who you *are* that counts," her mom said, "not what you look like."

*Sure*, Becky thought, *of course she can say that. She's as thin as a pencil.* Her dad was pretty heavy, but he was a historian. He sat in his study all day doing research and writing books. You couldn't expect him to look fit. She was surprised he appeared as healthy as he did.

"Well, I'm not a Hawaiian queen, so I've gotta lose weight," Becky said. Then, as always, she'd go to her room and call Kim, who'd tell her about the latest and greatest diet, where you only ate seaweed and guava salad.

"And besides getting thinner, it's really good for your skin!" Kim said enthusiastically.

"My skin is fine, Kim! I want to be thin."

"Then diet, Becky. But you know, it doesn't matter what you look like. It's who you are inside that counts."

6

Becky thought of all this as she walked into the locker room. She stopped and stared at the rows of girls, all of them thinner than she was; all of them, in her opinion, prettier than she was. And certainly more popular.

"Yeah, I know. It doesn't matter," she said under her breath, "unless you're in P.E."

# [2]

From: **Tereza**, tereza.ctmc@macnet.com.br
To: **Cyber.kdz**, thekids@cyber.kdz.net
Date: Tue, 17:28 (Tue, 20:28 GMT)
Subject: Fantastic News!

Queridos Amigos,

I have some wonderful news! In fact, I have LOTS of wonderful news! You won't believe it! Are you ready? Okay, here goes . . .

This comm is coming to you from a *PROFESSIONAL GRAPHIC ARTIST!* Yes, what you are thinking is correct. Your own Tereza, *a excelente artista grafica da Internet* (that's "excellent graphic artist of the wire," for those of you who don't live in Brazil), is now a professional! Here's how it happened.

Mama has a friend who started a new company that makes equipment for security systems. Alarms and cameras and electronic locks. He mentioned to Mama that he needed to have a logo made for his business, so she suggested me! (She is wonderful! And smart!) This friend, Sr. Faria, asked me to do a few drawings, and he liked what I did. So then we start to talk about payment. I was thinking I'd earn enough for all of us to have new PowerPC's! But I was very wrong. Because he is just starting the company, he doesn't have much money. And worse, the first batch of cameras he manufactured was defective.

Mama would never tell me what to do, but I knew from a few hints she dropped that maybe I needed to give Sr. Faria a break. But I had to get something for my work! Then I had a great idea. Sr. Faria thought it was great, too. My payment is 10 little video cameras! Like the ones you see up in the corner at the bank. Do you know what I mean?

Now, I do have to admit that they don't work. But I thought I could send them to Sanjeev and he could ask his parents to help him fix them. Then we can each have one of our own. What do you think of that? I don't know what we'll do with them, but I'm sure we can think of something! Let's hear some ideas!

Sua amiga,

---

From: **Josh**, joshthealien@aol.com
To: **Tereza**, tereza.ctmc@macnet.com.br
Date: Tue, 20:11 (Wed, 04:11 GMT)
Subject: Re: Fantastic News!

Tereza,

Congratulations on your very first job. The cameras sound great. I have an idea. Each of us can set the camera up outside our rooms pointed at the sky. Deeder and Sanj can write a JAVA applet to bring the feed into a Web page on CKServer. Then we can see the constellations all over the world anytime we want.

What do you think?

Josh the Alien

---

From: **Deeder**, rodan@netherspace.nl
To: **Tereza**, tereza.ctmc@macnet.com.br
Date: Wed, 07:43 (Wed, 06:43 GMT)
Subject: Totally Cool Idea

Hey TZ,

Great job! This sounds cool. Here's my idea. We create a computer security package. It comes with a camera and software that's like a pumped-up anti-virus program. When a diskette is put into a computer, it scans it for viruses. If it finds one it captures a shot with the camera. Then it automatically transmits the image to us and we know who was responsible for infecting the computer! Companies will be lining up for us to install this. We'll make a fortune.

Deeder
Protector of bits and bytes

---

From: **Sanjeev**, sanj!metalman@music.indiaU.edu.in
To: **Tereza**, tereza.ctmc@macnet.com.br
Date: Wed, 16:06 (Wed, 10:06 GMT)
Subject: very very cool

nice job, tz! i ran the idea past my parents and they said they would definitely help. mom is teaching a class on chip design so she might even make a class project of it at the university. free labor from students . . . that works! but she can only do that if the defect is in a chip. we'll get them working whatever it is.

i wanna mount a camera in garageland. it's a new club some university students started. they play metal, grunge, and the occasional riot grrrl disc. pretty cool place. if i can figure a way to hook the tube to the talkway i can check out the action right from my pc. everyone can find a music club nearby and do the same thing. especially josh. there are great clubs in seattle. we'll have the hottest bands live on the wire anytime!

did you get the recipe i sent you? there is no question but my mom's curry is the best there is. hot city! i still can't decide if i'm going to the university in comp science or heading to the mt. abu culinary institute. maybe i'll just start a band . . .

i've talked way too much.

---

From: **Tereza**, tereza.ctmc@macnet.com.br
To: **Sanjeev**, sanj!metalman@music.indiaU.edu.in
Date: Wed, 07:57 (Wed, 10:57 GMT)
Subject: Re: very very cool

Meu Querido Sanjeev,

I've never received an email from you with so many words! How talkative you've become. It would be a shame to not use that computer genius brain of yours in hi-tech, but if curry is what calls, you have to answer. I vote "no" on the band.

11

If you want to play music, try samba. That metal stuff is noise compared to a good Brazilian samba.

Um beijo,

P.S. I received the recipe but haven't had time to try it.

---

From: **Becky**, historian@nyc.net.us
To: **Tereza**, tereza.ctmc@macnet.com.br
Date: Wed, 16:31 (Wed, 21:31 GMT)
Subject: History in the Making

Tereza,

Fantastic news! Congratulations. Soon we will be seeing your artwork on the cover of international magazines. I know it!

Here's my idea. It's called Cyber.kdz World Archaeology.

Since all the Kids live in different parts of the world, we have the perfect way of sharing archaeological sites we would never get to visit. I don't know how to make it work but I'm sure Sanj and Deeder could figure it out. What I want to do is set up a camera to watch an archaeological dig in each region. I'm sure Josh could find a Snohomish Native American site near Seattle, and there are thousands of fantastic Indian shrines around Baroda, where Sanjeev lives. What do you think?

Becky

From: **Paul**, commx@nyc.net.us
To: **Tereza**, tereza.ctmc@macnet.com.br
Date: Wed, 16:54 (Wed, 21:54 GMT)
Subject: History . . . blech!

Dear Tereza,

Becky asked me to give you a message. She said to forget
about her idea because it is so stupid and boring. Boy! Leave
it to my sister to think of something lame like that. Waste a
good video camera on digging up old bones?!
Here is what we really need to do.
I've made up a game called Air Destruction. We're all flying
around in the air with jet packs on our backs. We have two
weapons: a sonic blaster (like the ones in Killer Missile
Attack) and 12 turbo-rockets. The jet packs are hard-wired
into our brains so we don't need our hands to fly. You win
the game if you blow everyone else out of the sky! Extra
points for the number of turbo-rockets you have left. Pretty
cool, huh?
The cameras are what makes it work. We set them up on a
special mount. Maybe Loren can design it. The cameras shoot
us and the program maps where our arms and legs are. Sanj
and Deeder can figure out how to make that work. But the
great part is that we're IN THE GAME! Moving our arms and
legs controls the images of us in the computer. We raise our
arms, we fly. We reach to the right, we grab a rocket.
Totally VR! I can't wait for this!
I'll send Sanj and Deeder all the game rules so they can start
programming. You can let the rest of the Kids know what
we'll be doing.

Commander X

From: **Loren**, loren.jouet@sun.com.fr
To: **Tereza**, tereza.ctmc@macnet.com.br
Date: Thu, 07:47 (Thu, 06:47 GMT)
Subject: Anniversary Celebration

Dear Tereza

My congratulations to you. To think you are a professional
artist! Fantastique! I am afraid it will be many years before I
can do any professional work. It is hard to get hired as an
architect when one is only 13 years old. Perhaps after I
attend the university, oui?

I know the cameras you speak of very well. They are often
used in elevators and my father sometimes must replace them.
The quality of the picture is not incredible, but it is not so
bad. And for the price we cannot complain. Here is my idea.

Cyber.kdz has been together for almost a year. In fact, it will
be our first anniversary soon. For me, the Kids are *mes
meilleurs amis*, my best friends. We have gone through much
together. You agree, I am sure. But I do not know any of the
faces of my friends. I think the first project with the video
cameras should be the creation of a Cyber.kdz Yearbook.
We can put our faces on the wire, secure in CKServer, and
know each other even a little better than we do now. Do you
like the idea?

Félicitations,
Loren

From: **Tereza**, tereza.ctmc@macnet.com.br
To: **Cyber.kdz**, thekids@cyber.kdz.net
Date: Thu, 20:06 (Thu, 23:06 GMT)
Subject: What to do?

Queridos Amigos,

I better find some more work quick. With all the ideas you sent me, we will need 20 more cameras! I've posted the ideas on CKServer. Check them out. We'll decide what we are going to do when we comm a week from Saturday.

I've sent the cameras to Sanjeev. When they are fixed, Sanj will ship them to each of you. Make sure he has your postal address! Talk to you at the comm.

Até mais,

# [3]

"Shut up."

Becky moaned as she reached out from under the covers, groping for the "sleep" button of her clock radio. She knew that if she found it, she'd get ten minutes more rest. Her head lay buried in the pillows as she reached blindly for the button. She knocked a book, her glasses, and the box of Kleenex to the floor before her hand finally landed on the clock.

"Shut up . . ." she mumbled again, as she hit the button.

Nothing happened.

Becky groaned. "Ohhhhh, it hasn't been three yet . . ."

But it had. Becky's alarm only let you hit "sleep" three times, then it made you get up and turn the little switch off on the side to silence it.

Becky let the music play. Even though it was a song by the Raving Fanatics—one of her favorites—she still wished she could turn the alarm off without opening her eyes. Because that meant she had to get up. And getting up meant she had to get dressed. And after she got dressed she'd have to eat breakfast. And after she ate breakfast, she'd have to go to school.

*School.*

She couldn't believe how much she hated it now. She used to like it. Elementary school had been great, and middle school had been pretty good. But high school was different. She had thought things were going to turn around after her great history presentation a week ago. But instead of getting better, the last week was the worst so far. It was even starting to affect her schoolwork.

She thought about what had happened in P.E. that day after history. She didn't want to think about it, but she couldn't help herself; the memories kept coming back.

Why did Jenny Sloat hide her gym shorts in the shower? Was it because Jenny had blown her history presentation just before Becky had aced hers? Was Jenny mad because Becky's presentation had gone so well? And did Melissa Marek decide to play "keepaway" with her shoes because she was Jenny's friend? But what about the girls she didn't even know? Why had they been so mean? Becky just didn't understand.

Not that she had thought about it *that* day. First she'd tried to ignore the taunting. Then she'd tried to reason with them. When that didn't work, she'd tried being mean herself. That had only made it worse. And then worse. And worse and worse. Becky couldn't even remember how it had ended, just Coach Kimball, her gym teacher, telling her she could leave early. She remembered throwing her clothes on in the empty locker room. Running away from school. Then walking, then running, then walking, through a world blurred by her tears. Coming home to an empty apartment. Throwing herself on her bed and sobbing. Kim was still at school, so she couldn't even call her. She had lain on her bed and cried her tears of loneliness until dinnertime.

"Becky! Are you up yet? You're going to be late."

Her mom's knock at the door brought Becky back to the present. She shook her head to dispel the memories, opened her eyes (painfully), and dragged herself out of bed and into the bathroom. She looked in the mirror and was surprised to see streaks of tears running down her face. She sighed.

"Okay, Beck, that's enough. You can do this. Think about Joan of Arc—she had it a whole lot worse than you . . ."

She washed up, got dressed, and walked into the kitchen. Paul and her father were sitting at the table.

"Where's Mom?"

Paul didn't look up from the back of the cereal box he was reading. Her dad answered.

"She just left. She had an early meeting before class."

"Oh."

Becky took a bowl down from the cabinet and then snatched the box of cereal from Paul's hand.

"Hey! I was reading that!"

"And now you're not," Becky replied, as she poured the flakes out.

"In a wonderful mood again, aren't you?" Paul said.

"Shut up."

"What's the matter?"

"I said shut up. Here. Keep reading." Becky shoved the box back into Paul's hand. Their father looked up from his book, an old, thick volume on Etruscan history.

"Is something wrong?" he asked.

"No, Dad," they chorused. They had learned long ago that though their father had the best intentions, it was easier to resolve their disputes themselves. If he helped, they usually ended up bored to tears during a long lecture about the benefits of the Venetian trade treaties of the Middle Ages, or William Penn's commitment to peaceful negotiation. Becky loved history but would rather read it herself. Paul hated it all.

"Everything's fine, Dad," Becky said. "Finish your breakfast."

Mr. Strahn turned back to his Etruscans and corn flakes.

"What's going on, Beck? You've been in a bad mood for months," Paul whispered.

"Have not. It's only been weeks."

"At least you've noticed."

"Of course, twitch-brain. I'm not stupid."

"Well, what's going on?"

"I don't want to talk about it, okay?"

"You don't have to bite my head off." Paul got up and put his bowl in the sink. "I'm outta here." He picked up his backpack and Gameboy. "Try smiling sometime, Beck. It won't break your face." The door closed behind him just before the cereal box smacked into it.

Becky's dad looked up. He stared for a moment at Becky, then at the cereal box lying on the floor next to the door, then back at Becky.

Becky shrugged. "Oops. It slipped."

Her dad sighed and returned to his book.

Becky's first-period geometry class didn't go too badly. No one bugged her and she got a B on her test. Second period was "Your Money and You." *Everyone* hated this class because it was so boring. You learned how to figure how much it was going to cost to send your kids to college in the year 20 zillion. Most kids were so concerned with doing their homework for their next class that they usually didn't pay any attention to the teacher . . . or Becky.

19

Third period was English with Mrs. Kalonick. The only problem Becky had in English was that Mrs. Kalonick didn't like her. But then, Mrs. Kalonick didn't like *anybody*. Still, Becky was a good writer and turned in her work on time, so she got pretty good grades.

At lunch, Becky sat alone reading, as always, in the corner of the cafeteria. She didn't mind that at all. Though she enjoyed talking to people, she *loved* books, which was why her second-favorite class was library science. She worked in the library right after lunch. She couldn't believe that she could get credit by spending time in the library. It was fantastic. Her favorite class, history with Mr. O, was sixth period. Then there was only the dreaded P.E. and she was done.

That's what school had become for her. Except for the few classes she enjoyed, Becky went through the day waiting until she could go home. Life was so different now from when she'd looked forward to school.

In the library, there was a backlog of books to be reshelved, so Becky spent the whole period doing that. Some of the students thought shelving was boring, but not Becky. Not that she was a big fan of the Dewey decimal system; she just loved handling books—the way they looked, the way they felt, especially the way they smelled. New books smelled sweet and crisp. Older books smelled a little musty and wise. And everyday there was that great feeling of discovery. There was a book about nearly everything! As she wheeled her cart from shelf to shelf, she loved the surprise of discovering that there was a book about glockenspiels. She had never even heard of a glockenspiel, and here was an entire book on how to play them. Or who would have thought there was a whole book about the spectacled *guillemot,* a bird that lives on the shores of eastern Eurasia? It was tough concentrating on her work and not sitting down to read each book before she found its place—its nest—along the long rows. Amid the towering shelves Becky felt hidden away, almost as if she were in a catacomb or a tomb. She was out of sight from the rest of the school, and the school left her alone.

When the period was over Becky walked quickly to Mr. O's class. They were studying Roman history. She loved to listen to Mr. O discourse on the problems of the Roman Empire and the similarities to the current issues in the United States: wasteful military spending and a senate that didn't care about the populace. It was one of his favorite topics, and he could talk about it for an entire period. Which he did. Most of the class seemed bored, but Becky sat captivated by Mr. O's intelligence and handsome smile.

When class finished, Becky gathered her books, took a breath, and prepared herself for dreaded seventh period.

"Becky, could you wait a minute?"

Mr. O beckoned from the front of the class. Becky walked to his desk and they both waited while the rest of the students filed out.

He put down his pad and leaned against the edge of his desk.

"Is everything okay with you?"

Becky was caught off-guard by the question. She stammered.

"Yeah . . . ah, sure . . . fine."

"You're sure?"

"Yes." Becky looked down.

"Because your scores on the last two pop quizzes were way down. That's surprising, coming from you. And when I see something like that, it usually means one of my students is going through . . . I don't know . . . something.''

Becky took a breath. Should she tell him? She glanced quickly at his face. He seemed so smart, so kind. He'd understand her problems.

But what could she say, *Oh, sorry, Mr. O. My test scores are down because I'm fat, everyone in P.E. teases me, I hate getting up for school, and it's affecting my classwork.*

Yeah, sure. She'd rather go through the Spanish Inquisition.

Becky shrugged. ''No, nothing's wrong . . . I guess I just didn't study hard enough.''

Mr. O looked at her intently. ''All right,'' he said slowly, ''but if something comes up, feel free to talk to me. You're an excellent student. I hold you to a higher standard than the rest of the class, you know. I don't want to have to fail you.''

Becky looked up sharply. Mr. O was smiling. It was just a joke.

''You'd better get to your next class,'' he added kindly.

''Oh, yeah, wouldn't want to miss that . . .''

Mr. O recognized the sarcasm in her voice but said nothing. Becky turned and left the room. She stared at the ground as she walked to P.E., thinking about Mr. O—glad at least one person at Bennington-Carver liked her.

# [4]

COMM TRANSCRIPT
COLLECTED BY CYBER.KDZ COMMBOT
TIME: 16:00 GMT (SATURDAY)
ONLINE:    TEREZA
           DEEDER
           LOREN
           BECKY
           PAUL
           JOSH
           SANJEEV
BEGIN TRANSCRIPT. . . . .

```
<Tereza>   Oi, everyone.
<Loren>    Bonsoir!
<Becky>    Hi everyone.
<Paul>     Commander X reporting in.
<Deeder>   Hallo
<Josh>     Hi.
<Sanjeev>  hey
<Tereza>   Before we get to the *real* important
           business, does anyone have anything?
<Sanjeev>  who's tried the curry recipe i sent out
           last week?
```

. . .
. . .

| | |
|---|---|
| &lt;Sanjeev&gt; | hey, what's up here? that's the best curry there is. get with it! |
| &lt;Tereza&gt; | I'm sorry, Sanjeev. I just haven't had time. Lots of schoolwork. |
| &lt;Loren&gt; | It is the same with me. I apologize. |
| &lt;Paul&gt; | I didn't want to try it. It sounded gross. |
| &lt;Tereza&gt; | Paul! |
| &lt;Paul&gt; | Well it did. I don't even know what curry is. I like macaroni and cheese. And root beer. And twinkies. |
| &lt;Loren&gt; | What is twinkies? |
| &lt;Becky&gt; | Never mind, Loren. Paul thinks he's funny. |
| &lt;Paul&gt; | Do not. It's true. I love twinkies! And ding dongs. |
| &lt;Loren&gt; | Ding dongs? |
| &lt;Paul&gt; | And sno balls. |
| &lt;Loren&gt; | What kind of food is this? |
| &lt;Becky&gt; | Disgusting junk food, Loren. I'm sure you don't want to know. |
| &lt;Paul&gt; | It is not disgusting! It's great! |
| &lt;Sanjeev&gt; | paul-dude, i thought we were friends. you're giving up my vindaloo curry for junk food? |
| &lt;Becky&gt; | Don't take it personally, Sanjeev. Paul really doesn't eat much normal food. If it wasn't for cereal he'd starve in a few days. |
| &lt;Sanjeev&gt; | c'mon, kids, someone's gotta try it. |
| &lt;Josh&gt; | We will, Sanj. We're not all good cooks like you. |
| &lt;Tereza&gt; | Anything else going on? |

. . .
. . .

| | |
|---|---|
| \<Tereza\> | All right. Now we get to the BIG topic: the Cyber.kdz video! What's the status on the cameras, Sanjeev? |
| \<Sanjeev\> | almost done. should be able to ship them out of here monday or tuesday. |
| \<Paul\> | Cool! Did you finish the programming yet? |
| \<Sanjeev\> | what programming? |
| \<Paul\> | Air Destruction! My game! I sent you and Deeder all the information. All you had to do was make it work. Is it done yet?! |
| \<Sanjeev\> | well . . . |
| \<Deeder\> | Paul, we haven't voted on what we're going to do. |
| \<Paul\> | Haven't voted? Why do we need to vote? My idea's the best. Everyone knows that. |
| \<Deeder\> | That's how we decide things, Paul. |
| \<Becky\> | Oh yeah, like the way you decided to go after those scum in New York last month? |
| \<Deeder\> | C'mon Becky. I was wrong to not listen to the vote, I said so. |
| \<Tereza\> | Deeder did apologize, Becky. We don't need the two of you fighting again. Paul, Deeder is right. We need to vote. |
| \<Paul\> | Arrgh! I can't even believe this! What's the matter with everyone? Did you read the other ideas? They're so stupid! |
| \<Tereza\> | Of course we read them, Paul. They're *our ideas*. |
| \<Deeder\> | Yeah, glad you liked them so much. |
| \<Paul\> | Well they're stupid! |
| \<Becky\> | Cool it, Paulie. |
| \<Tereza\> | Paul, if your idea is what everyone wants to do, then we'll all support it. We promise. |
| \<Paul\> | Oh great. But you'll probably want to do one of the stupid ideas. OW! |

```
<Loren>      Ow? What is ow?
<Paul>       That's what I say whenever Becky punches me
             in the arm like she just did!
<Tereza>     We don't need to get violent about this.
             Let's discuss the ideas and vote.
<Sanjeev>    yeah. let's do it.
<Tereza>     Does anybody want to say anything about
             their idea first?
<Deeder>     I hope everyone votes for my idea because
             it will stop a lot of scum and make us a
             pile of guilders.
<Paul>       What's guilders?
<Deeder>     That's Dutch money.
<Paul>       Just what I always wanted. Dutch money!
             That will do me a lot of good. OW!
<Becky>      Sorry everyone.
<Tereza>     Anyone else?
 . . .
 . . .
<Tereza>     All right, let's vote. We'll do it
             alphabetically. First is Becky's Cyber.kdz
             World Archaeology.
<Becky>      Me.
 . . .
<Tereza>     OK. Deeder's security program?
<Deeder>     Ja
 . . .
<Tereza>     Josh's World Constellation Web site?
<Josh>       Me.
 . . .
<Tereza>     Loren's Cyber.kdz Yearbook.
<Loren>      I vote oui.
 . . .
<Tereza>     Paul's Air Destruction.
<Paul>       My vote counts for 10 billion.
```

```
<Tereza>    Only one, Paul.
  . . .
<Tereza>    Sanjeev's Garageland.
<Sanjeev>   i vote for it.
  . . .
<Tereza>    And my idea for a Public Art Site on the
            Web.
  . . .
<Tereza>    Just me, I guess.
<Deeder>    That's a seven-way tie. This isn't going to
            work.
<Loren>     I have an idea. Why don't we make a rule
            that we can vote only for ideas that are not
            our own?
<Tereza>    That's good, Loren. Anybody have a problem
            with that?
<Paul>      Yes. I only want to vote for mine!
<Tereza>    Paul! We have to work together. Please try.
            Let's start again. Alphabetically, go.
<Becky>     World Constellation.
<Deeder>    Cyber.kdz Yearbook.
<Josh>      Cyber.kdz Yearbook.
<Loren>     Art Site on the Web.
<Paul>      I'm not voting.
<Sanjeev>   deeder's security program.
<Tereza>    I vote for the Cyber.kdz Yearbook. That's
            three votes for Loren's idea. Cyber.kdz
            Yearbook wins.
<Loren>     Fantastique. Thank you.
<Becky>     Wait! We should vote again.
<Tereza>    Why, Becky? That went fine.
<Becky>     No! I think we should. Loren's idea is just
            not interesting enough. We're the
            Cyber.kdz! We should be doing something
            incredible. Pictures of ourselves aren't
            that interesting.
```

| | |
|---|---|
| \<Josh\> | I like it. You're all my best friends. It'd be great to see all of your faces. |
| \<Deeder\> | Yeah, me too. It would be cool to put a face to all these words spinning across my screen. |
| \<Becky\> | We really need to do something else. Maybe we should do Paul's game. |
| \<Paul\> | Really? |
| \<Tereza\> | No. We voted already. |
| \<Becky\> | But Paul will feel really bad if we don't do it. Let's do Air Construction. |
| \<Paul\> | Air *Destruction!* |
| \<Deeder\> | You hate video games, Becky. What's going on? |
| \<Becky\> | I just care about my little brother. What's wrong with that? Let's do the game. |
| \<Sanjeev\> | i thought the game sounded cool. but it's a lot of programming. i don't have time for it right now. |
| \<Deeder\> | Neither do I. |
| \<Tereza\> | I don't know why we are talking about the game. We voted and Loren's idea won. |
| \<Becky\> | We should vote again. |
| \<Tereza\> | Why? Does anyone want to change their vote? |
| . . . | |
| . . . | |
| \<Tereza\> | See, Becky? |
| \<Becky\> | What about Deeder's security program? It's very good. We could make a lot of money. It would be exciting to go into business. It's a brilliant idea. |
| \<Deeder\> | That's the nicest thing you've said to me in a long time. Thanks. |
| \<Becky\> | I really think we should reconsider. |
| \<Loren\> | I do not understand this. But if you insist to vote again, then I will do that. |
| \<Sanjeev\> | i'm not changing my vote. i'm with the deedman already. cool idea. |

*28*

| | |
|---|---|
| \<Becky\> | Sanj knows what he's talking about. I think his vote should count for more since he fixed the cameras. |
| \<Josh\> | That's crazy, Becky. We always get one vote apiece! Why are you so against Loren? |
| \<Becky\> | I'm not against Loren. Don't think that. I love Loren. I just think we should do one of the other ideas. |
| \<Josh\> | Well I'm not changing my vote. |
| \<Deeder\> | I want to do my idea, but I can't vote for it. So I'm not changing mine either. You know, it's not like this is the only thing we're going to do with the cameras. |
| \<Tereza\> | Deeder's right. We'll do some of the other ideas after the yearbook is finished. |
| \<Paul\> | Yearbooks are dumb. I agree with Becky. We should vote again. But this time Air Destruction should win. |
| \<Sanjeev\> | hate to tell you this, paul-bud, but it ain't gonna happen. give it up. |
| \<Paul\> | You guys stink! I don't care anyway. I'm going to camp in a few weeks and won't even be around to play with the stupid cameras! |
| \<Deeder\> | Sounds like sour grapes. |
| \<Paul\> | Why don't you and Sanj make curry out of your stupid sour grapes? I'm outta here. |
| \<Tereza\> | Wait, Paul. Don't leave yet. Let's finish this off. This is supposed to be fun, not make everyone mad at each other. |
| \<Loren\> | C'est vrai. That is true. Let us vote again, if we must. |
| \<Josh\> | I don't think we have to. I've been keeping track and there aren't enough votes for any other idea to win. It's definitely yours, Loren. |
| \<Loren\> | Excellent! |

```
<Tereza>    Good. Then we're done. Loren, why don't you
            send out email to everyone letting them
            know what they should do?
<Loren>     I will. And you will help me with the page
            design, oui?
<Tereza>    Claro. Of course. Thought you'd never ask!
            I gotta go. Talk to you soon!
<Loren>     Au revoir.
[TEREZA HAS LOGGED OFF]
[LOREN HAS LOGGED OFF]
<Sanjeev>   oujo
<Deeder>    see ya
<Josh>      bye
[SANJEEV HAS LOGGED OFF]
[DEEDER HAS LOGGED OFF]
[JOSH HAS LOGGED OFF]
<Becky>     Well, it's just you and me, Paul.
<Paul>      Yeah. But we're sitting next to each other.
            We can talk instead of type.
<Becky>     I know.
<Paul>      Wanna?
<Becky>     I don't know.
<Paul>      Let's try.
[PAUL HAS LOGGED OFF]
[BECKY HAS LOGGED OFF]
COMM TRANSCRIPT COMPLETE
CYBER.KDZ COMMBOT TERMINATING EXECUTION
TIME: 16:21 GMT
```

# [5]

Paul pushed his chair back. It was such a pain that he and Becky had to share a computer during comms. Sanj wrote a little program that allowed each of them to log in to the comm from the same machine. They only had to hit Alt-P or Alt-B to toggle the screen back and forth depending on who was typing. And Deeder had sent them a little adapter so they could connect two keyboards. But they still had to jockey for position in front of the monitor. Most times there just wasn't enough room for the two of them—especially during heated discussions.

Becky pushed her chair back as well.

"I'm sorry your game didn't win," she said.

"Really?"

"Yeah, really."

"No, you're not," Paul said. "You're just sorry Loren's won."

Becky didn't respond. Paul was right. She couldn't argue with him.

"What's up, Beck? You love the Kids. Why don't you want to see what they look like?"

"That's not it, Paul." Becky closed her eyes. She didn't want to say what she was thinking.

"Then what?" Paul asked.

"I don't want to talk about it."

Becky started to get up. Paul grabbed her arm.

"Beck! This is Commander X you're talking to. I've saved your life about a zillion times in Galactic Starfighter. And you're not gonna talk to me?"

"Paul, I hate those games. I've never even played Galactic whatever. How can you save my life?"

"I named my Galactic Empress after you."

"Really?" Becky was touched.

"Sure. When you install it, the game asks you to name all the major characters. And as Commander X, it is my duty to serve and protect the Galactic Empress. So I named her Becky."

"Wow . . . that's really sweet . . ."

Paul smiled. "I know. Besides, the Galactic Empress is a four-headed Gargorian with scales and tentacles. It seemed like the right name." Paul scooted his chair back to be out of reach of Becky's fist.

But she didn't move; she laughed. She laughed for the first time in many weeks.

"You're crazy, Paulie."

"Call me Commander X, please"

"All right, *Commander X.*"

"*Now* what's up? Why don't you want to see the Kids?"

"It's not them, Paul. It's me. I don't want them to see *me.*"

The thought had been with her since she had first read Loren's idea over a week ago, but she'd never said it out loud. As the words came out of her mouth, the feelings she'd been holding back became stronger, more real. They rushed at her so quickly she couldn't stop them. Tears formed in the corners of her eyes. Her throat tightened.

"I don't want them to *see* me, Paulie."

"But the Kids love you."

"That's just it. They're the first friends I've ever had that don't look at me and think 'She's fat!' Except for Kim. And I don't get to see Kim much anymore. The Kids know me for who I am, not what I look like. They see the way I think, how I feel. They don't look at me with those cruel stares . . . like in P.E. They don't *know* what I look like. And I don't *want* them to. I don't want them to stop liking me."

"That's crazy. They wouldn't do that!"

"I don't know that. And I don't want to find out." The tears came now. *"I don't want them to hate me,"* Becky whispered.

Paul got up and walked over to Becky. He was four years younger and a lot shorter than his sister, but he was just the right size to put his arms around her shoulders as she sobbed sadly in her chair. He hugged her for a few moments without saying anything. The computer hummed quietly. They heard their dad's file drawer open and close in his office. The phone rang in the other room and they listened to the muffled voice of their mom answering it. Finally, Becky's tears slowed to a trickle.

"Beck, the Kids won't care."

"No, Paul. *They can't know.* You have to promise you won't tell them."

"But they'll see your picture."

Becky sat up. "Promise, Paul. Please."

Paul knew when his sister's mind was made up. There was nothing he could say to change it.

33

Becky looked at him. Her cheeks were marked with the tracks of tears.

"Please . . ."

"All right. I promise."

"Thanks, Paulie." Becky pulled him to her and squeezed. *"Thanks . . ."* she whispered.

"But what are you gonna do about the picture?"

Becky let go. "I don't know. I'll worry about that when I have to."

"Well, don't do anything weird. I know that will be hard for you . . ."

"Shut up, twitch-head." Becky reached for a Kleenex and wiped her eyes and cheeks. "You won't be here, anyway. You're going to camp."

"Oh yeah, I am! I can't wait! Camp SimBrain! Can you believe there really *is* a computer game camp?"

Becky rolled her eyes. "No, I can't. I mean it. And I can't believe Mom and Dad are letting you go."

"But they are! They are, they are!" Paul said in a singsong. "They have everything there: arcade games, computer simulations, even virtual reality! In the morning they have classes on how to code your own game. What a great way to spend spring break. Maybe I'll get to do Air Destruction . . . but it will be hard without Sanj."

"I don't think the counselors will be anywhere near as good as Sanj. He's definitely the best."

"Hey, I'll email you if the camp's on the talkway, okay?"

"Yeah, that would be good." Becky thought for a moment. "That'll be *weird*! I've never gotten an email from you before. We're always in the same place. It'll be a first."

Paul smiled. "Yeah! That's cool. I'll be able to call you names and not get punched!"

From: **Josh**, joshthealien@aol.com
To: **Sanjeev**, sanj!metalman@music.indiaU.edu.in
Date: Mon, 17:09 (Tue, 01:09 GMT)
Subject: What should I do?

Dear Sanj,

The camera arrived today. It looks great. I can't wait to try it.
But what am I supposed to do? There's a 16-bit card in the
box with the camera. I figured I should stick this in an empty
slot in my computer. But then what? Don't I need software?
What about IRQ conflicts? Let me know.

J

From: **Sanjeev**, sanj!metalman@music.indiaU.edu.in
To: **Josh**, joshthealien@aol.com
Date: Mon, 21:22 (Tue, 15:22 GMT)
Subject: Re: What should I do?

sorry about that, i didn't think the package would get to you
so fast. just finished the software. i'll be uploading it tonight

to ckserver.*ftp video.zip* in about an hour. it has all the files you need to get things going. instructions are included. irq conflict checker is part of the installation. should work fine. let me know if you have trouble.

---

From: **Josh**, joshthealien@aol.com
To: **Sanjeev**, sanj!metalman@music.indiaU.edu.in
Date: Tue, 20:53 (Wed, 04:53 GMT)
Subject: We Have Liftoff!

Cool! You must be an alien, Sanj. This stuff works great. Only took me 15 minutes to get it working. Which planet are you from anyway?

J

---

From: **Sanjeev**, sanj!metalman@music.indiaU.edu.in
To: **Cyber.kdz**, thekids@cyber.kdz.net
Date: Wed, 12:09 (Wed, 06:09 GMT)
Subject: it works

we got video! josh has his camera up and shooting. when you get yours, *ftp video.zip* from ckserver, unzip it, and follow the instructions. then start taking pictures!

---

From: **Josh**, joshthealien@aol.com
To: **Cyber.kdz**, thekids@cyber.kdz.net
Date: Tue, 22:35 (Wed, 06:35 GMT)
Subject: Sanj & Tereza Rule

Sanj and Tereza rule the wire. They are great! You can't

believe how cool this stuff is. Got the camera, loaded the files, and have already figured out how to shoot through my telescope. Got a great shot of Jupiter. You can even see the spots left from the Schumaker-Levy 9 comet crash. I'm going to really impress my astronomy club at our next meeting! Thanks!

---

From: **Tereza**, tereza.ctmc@macnet.com.br
To: **Josh**, joshthealien@aol.com
Date: Wed, 07:11 (Wed, 10:11 GMT)
Subject: Email Rules

Dear Josh,

I am very happy that you are enjoying the camera. I must point out the lack of a salutation *and* a closing in your last email. I'm sure it is because you were so excited. But I would expect that from Sanjeev and not from you.

Sinceramente,

From: **Josh**, joshthealien@aol.com
To: **Tereza**, tereza.ctmc@macnet.com.br
Date: Wed, 15:56 (Wed, 23:56 GMT)
Subject: Re: Email Rules

Dear Tereza,

I apologize.

Sincerely,
Josh

---

From: **Sanjeev**, sanj!metalman@music.indiaU.edu.in
To: **Josh**, joshthealien@aol.com
Date: Wed, 20:24 (Wed, 14:24 GMT)
Subject: who rules?

glad you're shooting, josh. spots on jupiter, huh? sounds cool.
bet you got nailed by tz on your last email. i'm right, yeah?

---

From: **Josh**, joshthealien@aol.com
To: **Sanjeev**, sanj!metalman@music.indiaU.edu.in
Date: Wed, 15:59 (Wed, 23:59 GMT)
Subject: Re: who rules?

Sanj,

  Yeah, you're right. She nailed me in about 5 minutes.
Sometimes I think she just sits at her computer waiting for
someone to forget a salutation!

Take care,

J

From: **Deeder**, rodan@netherspace.nl
To: **Cyber.kdz**, thekids@cyber.kdz.net
Date: Thu, 17:38 (Thu, 16:38 GMT)
Subject: Radical Video

OOOOOWWEEEEE! I never thought tv could be so fun! This
is cool stuff, friends. I got my video up and running and it is
great. I shot the cover of Kung Pao Chicks' last album and used
it for my screensaver. Then I figured out how to take a shot
whenever someone touches my keyboard. Here's the first one:

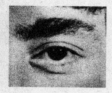

Tereza and Sanj RULE!

Video-Powered Deeder

---

From: **Sanjeev**, sanj!metalman@music.indiaU.edu.in
To: **Deeder**, rodan@netherspace.nl
Date: Thu, 22:50 (Thu, 16:50 GMT)
Subject: Re: Radical Video

sounds really cool, deedman. might want to move the camera
back a little.

From: **Sanjeev**, sanj!metalman@music.indiaU.edu.in
To: **Cyber.kdz**, thekids@cyber.kdz.net
Date: Thu, 22:54 (Thu, 16:54 GMT)
Subject: good way to celebrate

everyone seems to be pretty happy about these cameras. if
you really want to thank me, try making some curry to
celebrate. you have the recipe.

---

From: **Loren**, loren.jouet@sun.com.fr
To: **Cyber.kdz**, thekids@cyber.kdz.net
Date: Thu, 19:16 (Thu, 18:16 GMT)
Subject: Cyber.kdz Yearbook

Kids,

I am still trying to get my camera to work. We have to port
the software to UNIX for my SPARC system. In the meantime
everyone should create 6 pictures:

1. Portrait of your face
2. Picture of you standing up
3. Picture of you sitting at your computer
4. Your room
5. Your pet(s) (if you have any)
6. Your computer

When you are finished, put them in the YEARBOOK/PHOTO
dir on CKServer.
I will send the HTML pages to Tereza tomorrow so she can
add the graphics.

Start shooting!

Loren

# [7]

School. Gotta get up. School. *High* school. Don't wanna.
Gotta. School. No school. Not another day. No more
school. No more after today. Spring break. Last day of
school. *Last day of school!*

Becky opened her eyes. Last day of school? *What?*

She shook her head. Her clock radio had gone off and
was playing "Gazpacho Sunday" by the Veggimanics.
She shook her head again. What was she just thinking?
Or had she been dreaming? She couldn't remember.

Slowly it came back to her. She *had* been dreaming . . .
*She was lying in a nest made out of scraps of paper. Her
mom was shaking her trying to wake her up. She had to
go to school. But Becky didn't want to move. The papers
next to her head were pages from books and newspapers.
The closest page was a story. She began to read it. It was
about a beautiful princess named Kim who was famous
and . . . before she could finish, a gust of wind blew the
page away. Below it was a piece of newspaper. The head-
line screamed BECKY FAILS HISTORY BECAUSE OF
WEIGHT PROBLEM. She wanted to rip it up, but, it too,
blew away. Below that was another paper. It was a calen-
dar with today's date. Big red letters spelled, SCHOOL'S
OUT. Then her mom was shaking her again. . . .*

And then she woke. . . .

Becky's head began to clear. It *was* the last day of school—at least for a week. Spring break started tomorrow! That was something to look forward to. If she could only get through today, she wouldn't have to go back for a whole week.

*Okay, Beck* . . . she said to herself, *you can do it.*

She pulled herself out of bed, washed up, and dressed.

Her mother was standing at the stove, boiling an egg. Paul was eating cereal and her dad was chewing on a piece of toast with his nose in a book. A dufflebag and sleeping bag leaned against the wall in the front hall.

" 'Morning, sweetheart," her Mom called.

" 'Morning. What's all that?" Becky cocked her head toward the bags.

"My stuff," Paul said, not looking up from the cereal box he was reading. "I'm leaving for camp right after school. Hey! Did you know you can get a free VirtualMind game cartridge from Fruit Toots?!"

"Probably have to eat a ton of 'em," Becky said.

"No! It says here you just need to send in four coupons. I can eat four boxes of Fruit Toots in a day!"

"Let me see that." Becky grabbed the box and scanned the small print along the side. "You moron, Paulie. You have to send in ten tokens to get a coupon, and you only get one token in a box. You have to eat *forty* boxes!"

"I can do that." Paul grabbed the box and poured some more cereal into his bowl.

Mrs. Strahn walked over from the counter. "I don't think I want you to eat that much cereal, Paul. It's got a lot of sugar . . ."

"I *need* sugar, Mom. I'm a growing boy. I read an article in *GameQuest* magazine that said sugar speeds up reflexes. Eating a bowl of Fruit Toots can improve your score by ten percent in some games.''

Becky snorted. ''Yeah, sure. I wonder who paid to have that article written? Couldn't be the Fruit Toots Company, could it?''

''No way. They don't write articles. They just own the magazine.''

Mrs. Strahn shook her head. ''Regardless of what the article said or who wrote it, you're not eating forty boxes of cereal. Right, Johann?''

Mr. Strahn looked up from his book. ''Hmm? Did you say something?''

Mrs. Strahn opened her mouth to speak, but Paul interrupted her.

''Mom said I should eat more Fruit Toots so I'll be better at Galactic Starfighter,'' he said quickly.

''Well, if your mom says so, that's what you should do.'' Mr. Strahn turned back to his book.

Paul smiled. ''Even if it's forty boxes, Dad?''

Mr. Strahn looked up. ''Hmmm? Forty? Yes, forty is fine. Keep eating, Paul . . .'' He looked down again, brushed some toast crumbs from the page, and continued reading.

Mrs. Strahn smiled slyly. ''Well, someone has decided he doesn't want to go to camp . . .''

Paul's face went pale. His smile disappeared quickly.

''Just kidding, Mom. You knew that, didn't you? I don't even like Fruit Toots!''

Becky snickered.

''Shut up, pixel-pig,'' Paul said.

''I didn't say anything . . .''

Mrs. Strahn interrupted. ''That's enough. Now, finish breakfast and get going. Don't be late for school. You get

43

report cards today . . ." She finished her egg, wiped her mouth, and picked up her briefcase from the hallway.

"Oh great . . ." Paul grumbled. "I can't wait . . ."

"It better be good, Paul. Remember our deal—good grades or no camp." She kissed him on top of his head. "And no TV if you don't get at least a C average."

"How come you never tell *Becky* she can't watch TV?" Paul asked.

Mrs. Strahn kissed the top of Becky's head. "Because Becky hardly ever watches anyway. And she *always* gets A's. We never have to worry about her grades." She walked over to her husband, took a moment to try to straighten his hair, gave up, and then kissed him as well. "Becky cares more about her schoolwork than about electronic pocket games, like a certain someone. Goodbye, dear."

"Hmm? Oh, goodbye, Elaine . . ." Mr. Strahn mumbled, still reading.

Paul continued. "Becky does better at school because she's teacher's pet. That's not fair."

"You don't know what you're talking about, Paul," Becky said.

"Yeah, you are. Jeremy Sloat told me his sister's in your history class and the teacher is always talking about how great you are."

Becky looked down at her breakfast. "That's not true. And that's only one class," she mumbled.

Paul didn't stop. "Becky's got it easier than me, Mom. I shouldn't have to get the same grades she does."

"You don't, Paul. Everyone in this house is expected to get good grades. It doesn't matter if it's Becky or you . . . or me, for that matter. I expect myself to get the same good grades in my business classes. And now I have to go. I've got three meetings before noon. Love you!''

She hurried out the door.

Mr. Strahn closed his book. "I've got to drive downtown to the library today. Do either of you want a ride?''

"Sure," Becky said, jumping at the chance. Getting a ride meant she could avoid meeting her fellow students on the walk to school.

"Okay," Paul answered. He got up and put his cereal bowl in the sink.

"Paaaaaul . . .''

Paul turned. His dad was looking down at him with his hands on his hips, the way he did when Paul did something wrong. But he couldn't think what he'd done.

"What? I didn't do anything . . .''

His dad picked the cereal bowl out of the sink and set it on the table.

"You sit down right now. You haven't finished your cereal. Just because your mother left for work doesn't mean you can ignore her wishes. If she wants you to eat more cereal, then that's what you're going to do.''

Becky giggled. Paul laughed, too. Their dad looked bewildered.

"What are you two laughing at?''

"Nothing, Dad," Becky said. "Get your car keys. I'll make sure he finishes . . . every last bite.''

Becky waved as her dad drove away. She turned and walked the half block to school. As she entered the front door, the noise of the busy hall surrounded her. People were running back and forth, opening and slamming lockers, talking, and yelling. But there was more energy than

45

usual. It was the day before break, and everyone was pumped up.

Someone pushed her to the side.

"Watch out, piggy!"

"Oinky, oinky!"

It was the barbarians. The "junior barbarian club," as Becky thought of them—even though they were sophomores. Becky ignored them as they ran through the hall, causing problems for the more civilized students.

Becky walked through the crowds to her math class. In this part of the school, the hall was lined with tall glass cases filled with every yearbook Bennington-Carver had ever produced. Becky walked along staring absentmindedly into the cases. Smiling faces stared back at her. Hundreds of faces . . . thousands. All of them happy to have had their pictures taken.

*I hate yearbooks*, she thought. Thinking that made her think of Cyber.kdz.

*What am I going to do? I can't put my picture up on CKServer . . .*

Becky stopped. One of the faces had caught her attention. A page was open from a really old yearbook: 1977. She stared at a girl's face looking out from the dozens of photos that covered the page. The girl was smiling like all the rest. But what Becky noticed was that she was fat. You couldn't see her body, but you could tell. She had the same plump cheeks as Becky. And her chin was full. Her neck was too wide. Like Becky, she had brown hair cut to about shoulder length. This girl's nose was different and her eyes were darker, but still Becky knew what it must have been like to be in that body. At least, she thought she did. But why was this girl smiling? Becky leaned closer to read the small print under the picture:

**Martha Danforth**
**Most Friendly Girl**
**Class Vice President**
**Drama, Pep Squad, Honors History**

Most Friendly Girl? Vice President? Becky couldn't believe this. How could someone be popular who was so fat? Fat *and* loved history . . .

*Wow*, Becky thought. Slowly, a new idea began forming in her mind. Maybe she could make friends at school. Maybe she could be popular. And maybe the Kids wouldn't care how she looked. Martha Danforth had done it. Maybe she could, too.

Thinking that made Becky realize how accustomed to being an outsider she'd become since she'd started high school. In elementary school, she'd had lots of friends, not just Kim. She remembered their laughing and joking together at lunch. But now she spent every lunch period alone. On the subway Becky talked to whoever happened to sit down next to her. At school she only talked when answering questions in class. But it didn't need to be that way! Seeing Martha Danforth, the most popular girl of 1977, made Becky believe that.

*"If you could do it, maybe I can, too,"* she whispered.

"Talking to a relative, piggy?"

Becky jumped at the sound. She turned and found herself staring at the silver smile of Brad Sloat, one of the junior barbarians. Brad was Jenny Sloat's older brother, and he wasn't a nice guy. Becky figured that Brad was so mean because his mouth must hurt him all the time—it was filled to the gums with braces. The other junior barbarians were gathered behind him.

47

Becky found her voice. "What are you talking about?" she asked. "I'm not related to Martha."

"Martha! She's even given it a name!"

Becky was confused. What was he talking about? She turned back toward the case. On the shelf next to the '77 yearbook was a big piggy bank displayed there to commemorate a fundraising effort to buy new football uniforms. The junior barbarians thought she had been staring at the piggy bank.

Becky turned to walk away. Some of the lesser barbarians moved to block her path.

"What's the matter, oinky? Too smart to talk to us?" Brad said, his braces reflecting the fluorescent lights overhead.

Becky didn't say anything.

"Why do ya think you're so great, huh? You don't even belong at this school."

Becky still didn't say anything. She just waited.

"What's the matter, piglet? Nothing to say today? Guess you aren't so smart, after all. Why don't you just go back where you came from?"

Becky couldn't stand it any longer. She took a breath.

"I *am* smarter than you, Brad," she said, "*and* more civilized."

"Oh, she *speaks!*" Brad sputtered. "Miss C*ivilized*. Who cares? No one likes you anyway."

One of the junior barbarians spoke up. "Yeah. And you won't think you're so smart after today. Ha."

Brad looked around. "Shut up, Tim."

As Brad turned, a gap opened between him and the next boy. Becky shoved through it. She didn't run. She just walked fast, trying to ignore the insults that echoed in the hall behind her. She could feel the tears starting to burn at the corners of her eyes, trying to break free and roll down her cheeks.

*Don't. Don't. Don't,* she said to herself. She refused to cry. She would never give those jerks the satisfaction.

Becky was able to avoid the junior barbarians for the rest of the day. She attended her classes as usual and ate lunch alone. She was disappointed that there was a substitute teacher in history because Mr. O had left early for his vacation. She sat glumly while the sub presented a boring video. When it was over, the lights came on. There were only a few minutes left in the period. The sub reminded everyone that seventh period was canceled and they were to go to their homeroom to receive their report cards. Becky smiled. That was something to be glad about: no P.E.! She gathered her books and practically skipped to homeroom.

Unlike many other students, Becky loved getting report cards. She had always been a good student and she loved looking at the vertical line of A's broken by the occasional B. She sat at her desk as her homeroom teacher passed out the cards. Many students, dreading what was inside, put their cards into their packs without even opening them. But not Becky. As soon as hers was laid on her desk, she ripped it open.

She felt her stomach tighten. She felt dizzy. Something was wrong. She looked at the name across the top: *Becky Strahn.* It was hers. She looked down again. Something *had* to be wrong. But there it was. She looked at the name again. It hadn't changed; this was her report card. She looked at the grades again. They hadn't changed; it *was* her report card. It *was* her F. An F in history!

She felt dizzy again. And then she felt the burning at

the corners of her eyes. She heard someone snigger and looked up. No one was watching her. She looked down at the F again. What had happened? She felt angry. How could Mr. O do this? She felt a tear sneak out and start to make its way down her cheek. She heard someone snigger again. But when she looked up, no one was paying any attention to her.

She sat numbly until her teacher wished them all a good vacation and excused the class. Then Becky collected her books and walked out of the room. She didn't look at anything or anyone; she didn't pay attention to the yelling and jostling in the halls; she didn't hear one of the teachers ask her if anything was wrong—she just kept walking. Out the door, down the steps, and away from school. She swore she'd never go back.

# [8]

No one was home when Becky arrived. Paul's bags were gone from the front hall. On the kitchen table was a note from her mom and dad saying they'd taken Paul to camp and would be back for dinner. Paul's report card lay on the table as well: straight B's. Becky went to her room and dropped her books on her desk. There was a note there.

*My dear Galactic Empress,*

*I am off to improve my combat skills*
*so I can defend your empire. My shots*
*for the yearbook are in the CK dir.*
*Please upload them when you upload*
*yours. Thanks. See you in a week!*

*Commander X*

The last thing Becky wanted to think about now was putting her picture up on the Net. Maybe she should, though—just get it over with. A nice close-up of her big fat face with a caption under it:

51

**Becky Strahn**
**Most Miserable Girl**
**Couldn't Get Elected To Student Council If
    She Tried**
**Sits Alone At Lunch, No Friends, Failed
    History**

The Kids would kick her out of Cyber.kdz and it would be over with.

The doorbell rang. Becky didn't move.

It rang again. She still didn't move. She didn't feel like talking to anyone.

It rang again. Finally, a voice shouted, "Hello! Mr. Strahn! It's me, Kim! Can you hear me! *Hello!*"

Becky ran to the front door and pulled it open. Kim stood in the outer hall, her arms wrapped around her schoolbooks. She was surprised to see Becky.

"Beck, you're home! Wow! We got out early and I thought I'd get here before you and surprise you. When no one answered, I thought your dad was in his study reading and not paying attention, like he always does . . . you know how he is. Of course you do, he's your dad. But you're home! That's so great! I have so much to tell you. Can you believe it's spring break already? High school's the best! I got three A's on my report card, too! Isn't that great? I just love school! And Mom says I can go out for pep squad next year if I keep my grades up! *And* Justin Bradley wants to take me to the spring dance! Becky? Becky? What's the matter? *Why are you crying?*"

Kim dropped her books on the floor and grabbed Becky, who put her head against Kim's shoulder. She couldn't talk, she could only sob. All the misery of her year at school—all the teasing, all the loneliness, the F in history—everything came pouring out with her tears. Kim hugged her.

"Becky, Becky, come on."

They walked into the apartment with Becky still crying into Kim's shoulder. Kim shut the door behind them with her foot, leaving her books on the floor in the hall. When they got to Becky's room, they sat on the bed and Becky cried some more. Finally the tears slowed and Becky was able to talk.

And that's what she did. For the next two hours, she talked and Kim listened.

Finally, Becky had talked through all the sadness and she and Kim moved on to happier subjects. Soon they were laughing and joking, like they used to in middle school.

"What's this?" Kim asked, pointing at the camera mounted next to the monitor.

"That's a video camera. It takes pictures and stores them in the computer."

"Really? Neat! Can I try it?" Kim loved photography. She'd always said she wanted to be a model. She was the first one in any crowd to jump in front of a camera.

"Sure, if you want."

Becky flicked the power switch on the computer, turned the camera on, and took the lens cap off. When the computer had booted up, she started the video capture program that Sanj had written.

"Go ahead. It's all ready."

"What do I do?" asked Kim.

Becky laughed. How could Kim not know what to do in front of a camera?

"What do you mean? You pose!"

Kim laughed too. "No! I mean, how does it take my picture?"

"It's always taking your picture. See? You can see yourself in this window on the monitor."

Kim let out a little scream. "Ooooo! It's like being on TV." Kim waved at the miniature image of herself on the screen.

Becky continued. "And if you want to capture a single shot, you just press this key here. You can tell me when and I'll do it."

Kim reached over and turned on Becky's radio. The Raving Fanatics were playing.

"All right! My fave. Flex Careen is so cute."

Kim started dancing in front of the camera. Swaying back and forth, flicking her hair from side to side. Becky pressed the "capture" button every once in a while. Each time, a still image was displayed in a new little window on the screen. It was hard to hit the key just right so the picture looked good. Most of them looked silly, with Kim's hair stuck in her mouth, or her arm sticking out at a weird angle. But some of them looked almost like real model shots. Soon the entire screen was covered with images of Kim. Suddenly the computer started beeping.

"What's the matter?" Kim asked, still dancing.

Becky looked at the error message. "We're out of disk space. I guess these images use a lot of bytes."

The song ended and a commercial came on. Kim stopped dancing and sat down on the bed. She reached over to turn the volume down on the radio.

"Four-twenty! I can't believe it's so late! I gotta get home . . . my mom will kill me!"

She got up and gave Becky a hug. "This was really fun, Beck. Let's go to the movies on Sunday, okay?"

"Sure," Becky answered, and followed Kim out of the room.

Kim found her books still lying on the floor outside the front door.

"Oops. Glad these are still here!" She picked them up, gave Becky another hug and ran down the hall to the elevator.

"See you, Beck!" she yelled over her shoulder.

Becky closed the door. The house was silent except for the quiet jabbering coming from the commercial still playing on the radio. The apartment seemed very empty without Kim.

Becky walked back to her room and sat down at the computer. She deleted some of the really bad images of Kim until the "out of disk space" message went away. Then she turned the camera toward herself. Her image appeared in the main video window. She stuck out her tongue. Then she frowned. Then she stuck out her tongue again and tried to look cross-eyed, but not so much that she couldn't see the screen. That made her smile. She tried flicking her hair back, the way Kim did. She hit the "capture" key. Instead of looking fashionable, every image looked like she was being attacked by a dirty brown mop; these were nothing like the cool images of Kim that were scattered around the display.

In the bottom corner of the screen her mailbox alert was flashing. She hadn't called in to read email for a couple of days. Paul must have downloaded new mail before he'd left for camp. She double-clicked on the flashing icon. Her list of new messages appeared.

"Hmmmm, another threat from Sanjeev. Let's see what it says."

From: **Sanjeev**, sanj!metalman@music.indiaU.edu.in
To: **Cyber.kdz**, thekids@cyber.kdz.net
Date: Fri, 23:44 (Fri, 17:44 GMT)
Subject: growl

don't make me mad. i'm not sending these recipes out
because i want to clutter up the wire. someone's got to try
them. latest studies show that curry increases brain activity by
20%. be smart. eat it.


    Becky clicked the "delete" button. The next message
was displayed.


From: **Loren**, loren.jouet@sun.com.fr
To: **Becky**, historian@nyc.net.us,
   **Paul**, commx@nyc.net.us
Date: Fri, 20:01 (Fri, 19:01 GMT)
Subject: Photos s'il vous plaît

Dear Becky and Paul,

I've received the images from everyone else. Are you having
problems with the camera? If you are, Sanjeev will help you
fix it. Tereza has finished the graphics. I would like to have
the yearbook done by tomorrow night. It is Cyber.kdz's
anniversary. I only need the files from you two. Please send
them as soon as possible.

Merci beaucoup,
Loren

Becky clicked delete so hard she practically pushed the mouse through the desk.

"I don't want to send files, Loren!" she said out loud.

But she knew she should upload Paul's files. It wouldn't be fair, having everyone mad at him when he'd done what he was supposed to do.

Becky opened her FTP program. She highlighted Paul's files in the local CK directory and then connected to CKServer. After logging in, she selected the YEAR-BOOK/PHOTO directory as the destination. Then she hit the "copy" button.

She watched the status meter creep across the screen showing how many bytes had been transmitted. While she waited, she casually dragged the images of Kim around the screen. She lined them up so they made a perfect border around the edges of the display.

*I wish I could look like her*, Becky thought.

Her computer beeped, signaling that the file transfer was complete. Then it beeped again. And again. And then it played a few bars of the Raving Fanatics. A CKAlert message popped up:

*CKAlert from Loren. Please meet on Cyber.kdz Secure Line 2.*

Becky opened CK SecureComm. The login screen appeared.

---

>// Cyber.kdz Secure Line Login. Fri, 17:32
>// (Fri, 22:32 GMT)
>// Welcome, Becky. Enter Line Request: 2
>// Enter Password: ********
>// Who are you expecting to meet? Loren
>// Validation Complete. Line request accepted.

Loren:      Bonsoir, Becky.
Becky:      Hi, Loren.
Loren:      I was working on the yearbook and saw the
            files from Paul being transferred. I thought
            I would stop to say hello. We have not
            talked for a long time.
Becky:      Yeah, I know. Seems like all the Kids have
            been busy. We just got out of school today
            for spring break.
Loren:      Oh, c'est bon. That is good. Paul as well?
Becky:      Yeah. He already went to Camp SimBrain.
Loren:      Yes. I remember. You have strange camps in
            the United States.
Becky:      You're telling me . . .
Loren:      I like Paul but I do not understand his love
            for those games.
Becky:      Neither do I. I don't think anyone does. If
            he could, he'd play them all day. You
            should see what my parents have to do to get
            him to study.
Loren:      He stops playing long enough to study?
Becky:      Yeah. Mom and Dad said he couldn't go to
            camp unless he got a good report card.
Loren:      His grades were good then, yes?
Becky:      Good enough. He's gone.
Loren:      And did you get your grades?
Becky:      Sure.
Loren:      You're grades are good also, I am sure. You
            are very smart, I know.
  . . .

  . . .
Loren:      Hallo? Becky?
Becky:      Yeah.

| Loren: | Did I say something wrong? I am sorry. |
|--------|----------------------------------------|
| Becky: | No, Loren. You didn't. I'm just really upset. |
| Loren: | I can ask why? |
| Becky: | I got an F in history. |
| Loren: | WHAT?! C'est incroyable! This is incredible. I cannot believe it. You are a genius at history. |
| Becky: | No I'm not. I got a C on the last two quizzes. My teacher, Mr. O, said he was going to fail me if I didn't do better. And he did. |
| Loren: | But he cannot do that. It is not right. You should at least get a C! |
| Becky: | Mr. O said he holds me to a higher standard than the rest of the class. |
| Loren: | That is not fair. He could not have meant that. |
| Becky: | But he did. |
| Loren: | You are sure? Sometimes people, they joke and you do not know it. |
| Becky: | I thought he was joking when he said it. But I guess it was for real. |
| Loren: | What have your other grades been in this class? |
| Becky: | All A's. |
| Loren: | And for a few C's he fails you? I think something is wrong. What about your friends in class? Did they also get poor grades? |

. . .

. . .

| Loren: | I have said something wrong again? |
|--------|-------------------------------------|
| Becky: | It's not you, Loren. I'm just unhappy. The truth is, I don't really have any friends in history. No one likes me. |
| Loren: | This is hard to believe, Becky. You are so |

|         |                                                                 |
|---------|-----------------------------------------------------------------|
|         | friendly . . . except to Deeder.                                |
| Becky:  | Deeder's OK. We just get on each other's nerves sometimes.       |
| Loren:  | But why no friends at school?                                    |
| Becky:  | It's just high school. It's so different from middle school. You don't know what it's like. Everyone is really mean. |
| Loren:  | Mean? How are they mean?                                         |
| Becky:  | Well, they . . . I don't want to talk about it.                 |
| Loren:  | I am sorry.                                                      |
| Becky:  | Yeah. So am I.                                                   |
| Loren:  | Becky, I am thinking . . . are your report cards printed by hand, like they are in early grades, or are they done on a computer? |
| Becky:  | Computer.                                                        |
| Loren:  | And where is this computer?                                      |
| Becky:  | In the school office.                                            |
| Loren:  | Is it on the wire?                                               |
| Becky:  | I don't think so. The school is just getting connected. The computers in the library are on the Net, but I think that's all. |
| Loren:  | I see.                                                           |
| Becky:  | What are you thinking about, Loren? You want to get into the school's computer? |
| Loren:  | Perhaps.                                                         |
| Becky:  | Why? You're not thinking of trying to change my grade, are you? That'd be wrong! |
| Loren:  | You are right. It would be wrong. But I do not want to change it. I am thinking that maybe someone else has changed it. |
| Becky:  | That's crazy. Why would someone do that?       |
| Loren:  | Think, Becky. You are a genius when it comes to history. You get a C on two tests |

|          | and your teacher fails you. This doesn't make sense. |
|----------|---|
| Becky:   | But he said he would. |
| Loren:   | Yes. But you said he was joking. Now you think he was not. But then you tell me that there are many cruel students at your school. Everyone knows how important grades are. What is a terrible trick to play on someone? |
| Becky:   | Change their grades? |
| Loren:   | Oui! Yes! Change their grades. *You* think this Mr. O gave you the F because of his little joke about a higher standard. This *is* a joke, but a very mean one by someone else. |
| Becky:   | I can't believe that. |
| Loren:   | But you believe you deserve an F in history? |
| Becky:   | No. |
| Loren:   | I think the Kids should investigate this, Becky. |
| Becky:   | How? The computer's not on the Net. |
| Loren:   | If you get a copy of the database with the grades, I think Deeder can find out if there were changes made to it. |
| Becky:   | But how can I get it? |
| Loren:   | I don't know. That's up to you. Of all the Kids, you are the expert at sneaking into places. Just don't get locked in! |
| Becky:   | Very funny, Loren. I saved Deeder's life when I got trapped at Eastern SecureTech. |
| Loren:   | Oui, you did. You were fantastique. |
| Becky:   | Thanks. But I don't know if I can do this. I was lucky at Eastern SecureTech. I might not be this time. If I got caught sneaking into school, I'd be suspended. Or expelled. |

| | |
|---|---|
| Loren: | It is up to you, but I think you should try it. You cannot let this happen. You must stand up and fight back. |
| Becky: | I don't know. I'll think about it. |
| Loren: | Good. Let me know what you decide. |
| Becky: | I will. |
| Loren: | I need to finish up my work now. |
| Becky: | Thanks, Loren. It means so much to me that you care. |
| Loren: | It is easy to care about a friend such as you. |
| Becky: | Well, thanks for doing it. |
| Loren: | Before you go, I would like to ask you a favor in return. |
| Becky: | Sure, anything. |
| Loren: | Please send your pictures for the yearbook. I am excited about this and want to have it finished by tomorrow. |

. . .
. . .

| | |
|---|---|
| Loren: | I said something wrong again?! |
| Becky: | No. No, Loren. I'm sorry. |
| Loren: | You are sitting at your computer, yes? |
| Becky: | Yes. |
| Loren: | The camera is connected, yes? |
| Becky: | Yes. |
| Loren: | It is very easy to take the picture. You can send it to me right now. |
| Becky: | But . . . |
| Loren: | No. Do it. Then you won't have to worry about it and you will make me very happy. Promise me you will send a picture tonight. |
| Becky: | But . . . |
| Loren: | Please, Becky. |
| Becky: | All right. |

```
Loren:      Excellent. Merci, mon ami. Thank you, my
            friend.
Becky:      Sure. Talk to you soon.
Loren:      Au revoir.
>// CYBER.kdz Secure Line Closed
```

Becky stared at the screen. What had she done? She'd just promised to send a picture of herself to Loren for the Cyber.kdz Yearbook. What an idiot! What was she thinking? Everything was just so confusing. Loren's idea about someone changing her grade sounded crazy, but she wanted to believe it. And Loren was so nice; it was hard to say no to him when he asked for the picture.

The words on the screen jumped out at her:

```
Loren:     Promise me you will send a picture tonight.
Becky:     But . . .
Loren:     Please, Becky.
Becky:     All right.
```

A picture. A picture! She promised to send *a* picture. She shifted her eyes to the border of the screen. There, staring at her in neat rows, were a dozen pictures of Kim. She'd promised *a* picture . . . not *her* picture . . .

She clicked on another window; the one with the picture she'd taken of herself. The dirty mop was still attacking her head. She thought for a moment. There was no way she was sending that picture to Loren. But could she send a picture of someone else? Could she do that?

She clicked back to the picture of Kim dancing, looking like a fashion model.

Could she do it?

# [9]

Becky hadn't really planned on breaking into the school office.

At least, that's what she told herself.

She was just going to walk over to the school to see what was going on. Never mind that it was a Saturday.

And she just happened to slip a blank diskette in her pocket—just in case she decided to stop by the library on her way home and copy a few archive files.

It was a coincidence that the drab green army pants and t-shirt she chose to wear blended in perfectly with the hedges planted beneath the school's windows.

And the mini-binoculars her dad used at the symphony might come in handy if she decided to take up birdwatching suddenly.

She hadn't planned to break in.

But she did.

When she arrived at school she glanced around to see if anyone was watching. The coast was clear, and she quickly jumped behind the bushes that separated the building from the sidewalk. There was a narrow space about a foot and a half wide between the shrubs and the side of the building. She crouched down and slowly made her way along the wall, peeking into each window she passed. If the office was empty, she checked to see if the window was locked.

The bushes ended at the base of the steps that led into the school. Becky had checked every office. Each one was empty and dark, and every window was locked. There was no way in. She thought she might as well give up.

She stood up to squeeze her way out from behind the bushes. Just where the wall met the walkway, a water tap stuck out from the building. As she stepped over it, she lost her balance and the cuff of her pants caught on the faucet's knob. She fell forward with an "ooomph," her pants twisting the faucet and starting the water flowing—right into her shoe. She let out a sigh. Her shoe was full of cold water, her face was on the dirty walkway, and branches were poking her in the butt.

"Becky Strahn? Is that you, Becky?"

Becky twisted and looked up. It was Ms. Alexander, her geometry teacher.

"What are you doing? Are you okay?" Ms. Alexander leaned over and held out a hand. Becky took it, stood up and brushed herself off.

"Oh, hi, Ms. Alexander . . ." Becky fidgeted. Her right shoe squished as she shifted her weight onto it. Ms. Alexander looked down at the puddle under Becky's foot.

"What are you doing?" she asked slowly. Becky thought she heard the edge of suspicion in her voice.

"Ah . . . oh . . . I'm, a . . . ahh . . ." Becky's hand brushed the mini-binoculars that were hanging around her neck. "I'm birdwatching!"

"Really? Here?"

"Oh, yes! It's fantastic around here. Didn't you know?

I'm very interested in it. There have been reports that a spectacled sphinx has been spotted!''

"Spectacled sphinx? Is that a real bird?'' Ms. Alexander looked around skeptically. She was a great math teacher but she had no idea about anything in nature.

Becky answered hurriedly. "Oh, yeah. Of course, that's its nickname. It's really the purple-beaked spectacled guillemot, but because it's so, ah . . . so, ah . . . so hard to find, we call it the spectacled sphinx because . . . you . . . ah . . . practically have to go to Egypt to see one! Ha ha. That's a little birdwatching humor.'' Becky looked up at her math teacher and smiled.

Ms. Alexander smiled back, amused. "If you say so. I didn't know you were interested in birds, Becky . . . oh, where's that water coming from?''

The tap was still running and a small stream was pouring from the bushes onto the walkway. Becky steadied herself against the wall, leaned over, and turned it off.

"That was really stupid of me!'' Becky rolled her eyes trying to be cute. "I thought I saw that sneaky bird behind the bushes, but it wasn't him. It turned out to be an elementary warbler.''

Ms. Alexander looked skeptical again. Becky waved her hand casually and continued.

"You see them around all the schools. Very plain birds. Anyway, when I was trying to get out from the bushes, I tripped on the water tap. I was having a little problem when you found me. Ha ha.'' Becky smiled again. Ms. Alexander smiled, too.

"Well, you look quite a mess now. You should get cleaned up. I'm picking up a few things from my classroom. If you want, you can use the faculty washroom.''

Becky *didn't* want to. She just wanted to be gone. She

felt like a complete idiot standing in front of her teacher with her clothes covered in dirt and her shoe full of water.

"Oh, no thanks, Ms. Alexander. I'll just head on home. Guess I'll have to find that bird another day. Ha ha."

Ms. Alexander felt sorry for Becky and wouldn't take no for an answer. She gently grabbed her arm and pulled her toward the front door.

"Come along. At least you can use some paper towels to dry out your shoe." She smiled again. "You can't go squishing all the way home. It's chilly out."

Becky relented. "Okay. I'll hurry, though."

She followed her teacher up the few steps and waited as Ms. Alexander unlocked the door. Once inside, her teacher pointed to the faculty washroom. "Right in there. I'll just be down the hall in my class."

"Thanks, Ms. Alexander."

Becky pushed through the door. Inside, she took off her tennis shoe and tried to squeeze it out as best she could. She used some paper towels to absorb the water that had soaked into the sole. She wiped most of the dirt off her clothes and then washed her face.

The hall was empty as she walked out of the washroom. She could see Ms. Alexander's open classroom door at the far end. It was weird, being in the hall with no one else. It was usually so crowded with kids pushing and yelling. She walked down to Ms. Alexander's classroom, her footsteps echoing in the empty corridor. Ms. Alexander was going through some papers on her desk.

"Thanks, Ms. Alexander. I appreciate it."

"No problem, Becky. You watch out. Don't get caught by one of those water-billed faucet birds!" Ms. Alexander smiled at her joke.

67

Even though it was kind of stupid, Becky laughed to be polite.

"Ha! That's a good one. I won't get caught! See you."

"Have a good vacation."

Becky walked back down the hall. On her left, across from the faculty washroom, behind large panes of glass, was the school office. The lights were off, but Becky could make out the secretaries' desks, the door to the principal's office, and there, in the far corner, the dim outline of a computer.

When she reached the front door, Becky stopped and looked back. The idea popped into her head so fast she didn't have time to talk herself out of it. She pushed the door all the way open, took a step back into the building, and let it swing shut. The clang reverberated through the hall. She tiptoed across to the washroom, carefully opened the door, and crept inside. Then she hurried into one of the stalls and sat down.

After Becky had checked her watch for the twentieth time, she was sure time had stopped. Why wasn't Ms. Alexander leaving? Was she going to spend her whole vacation here? After ten minutes (which seemed liked ten hours), Becky heard the sound of a classroom door closing, then footsteps growing louder in the hall. She waited to hear the front door open and shut. But instead, she heard the washroom door open! She had only a moment to grab her knees and pull her feet up onto the toilet seat.

There were two stalls. Becky had a fifty percent chance of being discovered. She had taken the stall farther from the door. Did that improve her chances? What if Ms. Alexander had a favorite stall and it was the one Becky was in? Then it didn't matter that there was an empty one. And what would she say if she were found? She couldn't tell Ms. Alexander that she was birdwatching in here! Maybe she could. The brown-footed tile lark?

All this shot through Becky's mind in the four seconds it took Ms. Alexander to open the door, walk across the washroom, and grab the stall handle. Becky shut her eyes.

"I wonder how many tiles there are in this floor."

Ms. Alexander went into the stall next to Becky's. She was talking to herself as she went to the bathroom!

"Hmm . . . three-inch tiles . . . four per foot . . . about eight feet by ten feet . . ."

Becky bit her lip to keep from laughing. Her teacher continued.

"32 times 40 . . . One thousand . . . two hundred and eighty. That's about right."

Ms. Alexander flushed the toilet and opened the stall door. She chuckled to herself.

"Heh, heh. Water-billed faucet birds! That's very funny!"

She washed her hands and finally left the washroom. Becky didn't breathe until she heard the front door slam shut. Then she laughed really hard.

"Water-billed faucet birds! She's crazy!"

She went to the washroom door and cracked it open. She couldn't see much and she heard nothing. She opened the door farther and stuck her head out. The hall was empty. Through the glass front doors she saw Ms. Alexander crossing the street. She waited until her teacher was out of sight and then ran across the hall. The door to the office was locked.

"Darn!" Becky looked for another way in.

The next door down led to the teachers' staff room. She tried the knob. It turned.

The staff room had a few large tables surrounded by

chairs. The walls were covered with flyers announcing meetings, health plan changes and credit union services. There were lots of pro-education posters, too. One said, *If they've gotta go to school, they've gotta have a school to go to.* Another read, *Making the grade doesn't have to be an uphill battle.*

Toward the back were several other doors. Becky tried these. One was a closet. One was a supply room. A third led into a small room with a copy machine. This room had another door on the opposite side. Becky tried it.

It opened. She was looking into the school office.

*Boy, am I getting good at this or what?* she thought. *Maybe I should be a corporate thief . . . seems like all I'm doing these days is sneaking around offices.*

She quickly made her way through the maze of desks to the computer. Reaching around the side of the box, she flicked the switch and the CPU's fan began to whir. The monitor hummed and started to glow.

It was DOS based, and that was good. She didn't have to try to remember those crazy grephead UNIX commands Loren had taught her. A menu popped up. There were quite a few selections, but the one she wanted was obvious: GRADES DATABASE. She down-arrowed the selection and hit <Enter>, then waited for the program to load. She heard a noise and spun around. Through the glass wall she saw that the hall was empty. She heard the noise again and turned to see a telephone answering machine on one of the desks click on and then off. She was jumpy. She had to get out of there fast.

The program finished loading and she quickly scanned the menu choices. Under MAINTENANCE she found what she was looking for. She selected BACKUP DATABASE. The disk drive whirred. The computer beeped and displayed an error message:

THERE IS NO DISK IN DRIVE A. INSERT DISK AND TRY AGAIN.

Becky reached into her pocket and found the diskette. She shoved it into the drive slot and hit <Enter>. The computer chugged away as it began copying files.

Again time seemed to creep by. Becky counted the clicks of the disk drive, hoping to hear them stop. She looked over her shoulder at the empty hallway.

"Come on!" she insisted.

Finally the whirring drive fell silent. BACKUP COMPLETE appeared on the display. She exited the program, popped the disk out, and flipped the power switch off.

*I should definitely think about corporate espionage,* she thought.

She turned to head out the door to the copier room but stopped. What if Deeder needed more information? She couldn't count on Ms. Alexander letting her in again. Quickly she scooted between the desks to the principal's office. She pulled the louvered blind up a little and flicked the window catch open. Then she let the blind down and left.

Once in the hall, she carefully looked outside. No one was around. She pushed through the doors and ran around the side of the building. When she was away from the school she slowed and casually walked down the sidewalk, her hand tightly wrapped around the diskette in her pocket. Her shoe was a little bit squishy and her foot was cold, but Becky didn't care. She was in a good mood. That was the most fun she'd had at school in a long time.

# [10]

---

COMM TRANSCRIPT
COLLECTED BY CYBER.KDZ COMMBOT
TIME: 17:00 GMT (TUESDAY)
ONLINE:   DEEDER
          BECKY
          TEREZA
          JOSH
          LOREN
          SANJEEV
BEGIN TRANSCRIPT. . . . .

<Tereza>   Hi, friends. Everyone here?
<Loren>    Oui
<Becky>    Hi!
<Josh>     Hey
<Deeder>   Yo!
<Sanjeev>  kemcho
<Tereza>   Where's Paul?
<Becky>    He's at camp.
<Tereza>   Oh, that's right. Let's get started. We
           have a lot to talk about.
<Deeder>   You got it! Big stuff!
<Becky>    You had a chance to look at the database,
           Deeder?

| | |
|---|---|
| \<Deeder\> | What do you think?! This ain't a virus, but the next best thing! |
| \<Becky\> | What do you mean? |
| \<Deeder\> | Scum come in different flavors. I prefer to go flu-hunting. But if there isn't a virus around, well, database-tampering scum are almost as good. |
| \<Becky\> | You mean the database was tampered with? |
| \<Deeder\> | You got it, Beck! You've been set up. |
| \<Tereza\> | Are you sure? |
| \<Deeder\> | Not totally. But I'm pretty sure. |
| \<Sanjeev\> | give us the details. |
| \<Deeder\> | After Becky sent me the file I had to figure out its structure. That wasn't so hard. It turned out to be an old qBase format. Not a problem. So I started picking through it. But I got bummed real quick. |
| \<Sanjeev\> | how come? if you can read the format you just gotta look at the *last_updated_by* field. |
| \<Deeder\> | No way, man. You forget, this machine wasn't on the wire. It's not multiuser—you don't log in to it. It doesn't know who is punching the keys. |
| \<Sanjeev\> | you're right, dude. |
| \<Josh\> | What did you do? |
| \<Deeder\> | First I beat my head against the wall for a while. Then I put on some Kung Pao Chicks really loud. That's a trick I learned from Sanj. Helps me think. Finally I got it. Hidden deep in the data structure are a couple of encrypted fields that are used by the database system to keep the files from getting corrupted. They keep track of indices and stuff like that. One of these fields has the date and time every record |

73

|           |                                                              |
|-----------|--------------------------------------------------------------|
|           | was last changed. So I cranked up Godzilla and broke the encryption. Then I sorted all the records based on the date. And guess what? |
| \<Josh\>    | Becky's F was the last one changed? |
| \<Deeder\>  | Not exactly, Alienman. But it was one of the last. So I had to find out some more. Turns out that qBase programs build a backup table so any changes made to the database can be reversed in case an error occurs. |
| \<Josh\>    | So when the grade was set to an F, this table kept a record of what it was before the change? |
| \<Deeder\>  | Yeah, that's right. |
| \<Tereza\>  | What did Becky really get? |
| \<Deeder\>  | Do we even have to ask? Becky leaps to the head of the class with an A+! |
| \<Sanjeev\> | wait a sec. why does this mean someone screwed with the data? |
| \<Deeder\>  | Don't you see, Sanj? Becky had an A+ and someone changed it to an F. |
| \<Josh\>    | Makes sense to me. |
| \<Sanjeev\> | but maybe becky's teacher changed it. |
| \<Tereza\>  | Sanj is right. |
| \<Loren\>   | Yes. You said other grades had been changed as well. |
| \<Deeder\>  | But from an A+ to an F? C'mon! You know scum are at work here. |
| \<Becky\>   | I want to believe you so much, Deeder, but I'm not sure. My teacher did threaten to fail me. |
| \<Deeder\>  | Yeah, but Loren said that was just a joke. |
| \<Tereza\>  | Whether it was or not, I don't think we have proof that someone besides the teacher actually changed Becky's grade. |

| | |
|---|---|
| &lt;Loren&gt; | I agree. |
| &lt;Josh&gt; | So what do we do now? |
| &lt;Becky&gt; | I don't know. I guess I can ask my teacher about it when we go back after vacation. |
| &lt;Deeder&gt; | Whoa! Wait a sec! What's he going to do? |
| &lt;Becky&gt; | Fix it. He'll give me my A. |
| &lt;Tereza&gt; | A-PLUS! |
| &lt;Becky&gt; | Yeah. I'm sure it won't be a problem if I wasn't supposed to get an F. |
| &lt;Deeder&gt; | But it's already a problem! What about the scum who did this? |
| &lt;Becky&gt; | We don't know there are any scum, Deeder. |
| &lt;Deeder&gt; | But there might be! That's the point. If your teacher just changes it back to an A then the scum gets away. |
| &lt;Sanjeev&gt; | you got some kind of a plan, dude? |
| &lt;Deeder&gt; | What do you think? If scum are involved, I'm not going to rest until we nail them. |
| &lt;Becky&gt; | Wait a minute, Deeder. I don't want to get all involved in some crazy chase. My grade will be fixed and that will be enough. |
| &lt;Deeder&gt; | No, it's not! We can't let people go around thinking that computers can be used like that. If these scum get away with this, then they'll think they can get away with more. We have to stop them now! |
| &lt;Sanjeev&gt; | deed's right. nail 'em so they get the message. |
| &lt;Loren&gt; | Je suis d'accord. I agree. |
| &lt;Tereza&gt; | I'm not sure I agree, but let's hear your plan, Deeder. |
| &lt;Deeder&gt; | This is it. There's no way to figure out who is using this computer because it's a stand-alone machine. And we can't monitor it because it's not on the wire. So the only way to smear these scum is to catch them in the act. |

| | |
|---|---|
| \<Josh\> | That would mean watching the computer 24 hours a day. |
| \<Deeder\> | You got it, Alien-dude. |
| \<Josh\> | How can we do that? |
| \<Deeder\> | Thanks to our very own *professional* graphic artist and the Cyber.kdz techno-guru, we have a bunch of video cameras. All we do is write a program that triggers the camera to take a shot whenever the grades database is changed. I've written a lot of the code already. Then we hide a camera nearby and the spy-cam program clicks away. Every couple of days we copy the pictures to disk and soon we have what we need: proof! Put the photo and database log on a disk, mail the package to the principal, and watch the scum crash big-time. |
| \<Loren\> | That is a great idea, Deeder. |
| \<Deeder\> | Yeah, I know. |
| \<Sanjeev\> | but dude, those graphic files take a lot of disk space. it could easily max out the hard drive. |
| \<Deeder\> | We just need to keep taking the files off the disk every couple of days. |
| \<Sanjeev\> | that's cool. just have to make sure to delete the old files after they're offloaded. |
| \<Josh\> | This is cool! I like it. |
| \<Tereza\> | It is a good idea. |
| \<Deeder\> | Thank you, thank you. I wish I could hear the applause . . . |
| \<Becky\> | WAIT A SECOND! You're forgetting something! |
| \<Tereza\> | What, Becky? |
| \<Becky\> | We've got to get this program *on* the computer and hide the camera somewhere in the office. *And* someone has to get in there every few days to offload the pics. |

```
<Deeder>     I didn't forget that. That's your job.
<Becky>      MINE?
<Deeder>     Sure. Who's the expert at breaking into
             offices?
<Josh>       Becky!
<Deeder>     Who's got the most experience in on-site
             corporate espionage?
<Loren>      Becky!
<Deeder>     Who already got into the building so she
             could copy the database?
<Tereza>     Becky!
<Deeder>     And who's the only member of Cyber.kdz
             currently in New York?
<Sanjeev>    becky
<Deeder>     You're it, B!
<Becky>      But we aren't even sure someone changed the
             grade. What if I really got an F?
<Deeder>     Maybe you did. But if you didn't, then this
             will stop the scum from doing any more damage.
<Josh>       Yeah, Becky. C'mon. It'll be fun. You told
             me you had a good time getting in to copy
             the database.
<Becky>      I know. You're right, Josh. All of you are.
             But it's one thing getting in once more to
             set up the camera. How am I going to sneak
             in every couple of days to copy the files to
             diskette?
<Deeder>     You'll have to figure that out yourself.
<Becky>      But there's almost always someone in the
             office when school's in session.
<Deeder>     Sneak in at night.
<Becky>      Sure. Like I'll just tell my parents I'm
             going for a stroll at 1 A.M.!
<Sanjeev>    i do.
<Becky>      That doesn't surprise me. You're weird
             anyway, Sanj. And I mean that in a good way.
```

77

```
<Sanjeev>  what other way could you mean it?
<Josh>     Wait a sec. Becky, does the computer have a
           modem?
<Becky>    I don't know. Let me think . . . I don't
           remember seeing one, but there might be.
           There probably has to be. I think it dials
           the district office for budget stuff. We
           talked about that when we learned about
           budgets in Your Money and You.
<Sanjeev>  what's that?!
<Becky>    Never mind, Sanj. You wouldn't like it.
<Josh>     If there is a modem then why can't the spy-
           cam program transfer the files to CKServer
           at night?
<Deeder>   No reason! Great idea. It wouldn't be hard
           to code. Sanj?
<Sanjeev>  no prob.
<Tereza>   What about security? The spy-cam program
           would need to log in. Wouldn't it be
           dangerous having a CKPassword hanging out
           on an unattended computer?
<Sanjeev>  that's smart, tz. but the deedman can
           encrypt it before we compile. and we can
           set up a temp account on ckserver. as soon
           as we nail the scum we'll cancel it.
<Tereza>   Great. What do you say, Becky?
<Becky>    What can I say? These tech-brains have
           covered all the bases. All I have to do is
           plug in the camera. After sneaking into the
           school office for a second time, of course!
<Deeder>   Gaaf!
<Josh>     Gaaf? What's gaaf?
<Deeder>   It means ``cool'' in Dutch.
<Josh>     Oh. Gaaf!
<Becky>    So when do we do this?
<Deeder>   Sanj and I have to comm and figure out how to
```

|            | write the spy-cam program. Then we'll send you everything you need. |
|------------|---------|
| \<Becky\>  | You should hurry. School starts in 6 days. I'll need to set it up before then. When the principal comes back, he'll probably lock his window. |
| \<Tereza\> | What are you talking about, Becky? |
| \<Becky\>  | Well, when I was copying the database I did do one other thing before I left. |
| \<Tereza\> | You didn't . . . |
| \<Becky\>  | I did. I unlocked the window to the principal's office. |
| \<Deeder\> | SNEAK! You were planning to get back in all along! |
| \<Becky\>  | I wasn't sure! It was a ''just in case'' move. You know. |
| \<Josh\>   | Yeah, we believe you, Becky. Or should we call you Agent Strahn? |
| \<Becky\>  | ''Becky'' will be fine. |
| \<Deeder\> | Sanj, let's meet on the beam tomorrow and get the spy-cam prog rolling. |
| \<Sanjeev\>| sounds good, deed. |
| \<Tereza\> | I think that closes that matter for tonight. Let's move on. I think we all need to say thanks to Loren for creating a great yearbook. |
| \<Josh\>   | Really neat, Loren. Thanks. |
| \<Deeder\> | Excellent, man. |
| \<Sanjeev\>| total. |
| \<Loren\>  | Wait! It was not just me. Thank you to Tereza for the graphic design and to all of you for the pictures. They are fantastique! |
| \<Josh\>   | They *are* great! Hey, Sanj, you look pretty wild with that crazy hat on your head. |
| \<Sanjeev\>| that's a fez. pretty cool, huh? my cousin brought it back from turkey. it helps me think. |

| | |
|---|---|
| \<Josh\> | I bet! As long as you don't look in the mirror. Then it will help you laugh. It's pretty funny. |
| \<Sanjeev\> | not as funny as your t-shirt. |
| \<Josh\> | What are you talking about? |
| \<Deeder\> | You know what he's talking about, Josh. That t-shirt is so lame. |
| \<Josh\> | Is not. |
| \<Deeder\> | C'mon! ''Astronomers have stars in their eyes''? Boy, is that bad! On what planet do they think that's clever? |
| \<Josh\> | It's my astronomy club t-shirt. That's the slogan we picked! |
| \<Tereza\> | Don't get upset, Josh. We love you anyway. |
| \<Josh\> | Well I wouldn't talk, Miss Dorky Smile. |
| \<Deeder\> | Ha! That's funny! |
| \<Tereza\> | What's funny? |
| \<Deeder\> | Josh got you, Tereza. Your smile does look dorky. I like that word, Josh. Dorky! |
| \<Tereza\> | It does not! |
| \<Loren\> | I must say that it does. |
| \<Sanjeev\> | what were you doing, tz? did you get some superglue stuck on your lips? |
| \<Tereza\> | That's not fair. I tried hard to get my smile just right. |
| \<Josh\> | You look kinda sneaky to me. |
| \<Deeder\> | Sneaky . . . and dorky! |
| \<Tereza\> | I was trying to imitate the smile of the Mona Lisa. That is the most famous smile in the world. On the most famous painting in the world. |
| \<Josh\> | Maybe you should leave it on the painting. It looks better there. |
| \<Tereza\> | You guys are terrible! |
| \<Josh\> | Don't take it personally, Tereza. We still love you. |

| | |
|---|---|
| \<Deeder\> | Even though you have a dork smile! Ha ha! |
| \<Tereza\> | Don't laugh too hard. You might hurt your neck . . . |
| \<Deeder\> | What are you talking about? |
| \<Tereza\> | It's just that, well, how can I say this? You look a bit like a giraffe, Deeder. |
| \<Josh\> | He does look like a giraffe! |
| \<Deeder\> | What is with you two? I don't look like a giraffe! |
| \<Tereza\> | Oh yes you do. With that bandanna tied around your neck. It makes your neck look really long. |
| \<Deeder\> | I like my bandanna. It's cool. |
| \<Josh\> | Cool if you're a giraffe. A gaaf giraffe! |
| \<Sanjeev\> | i think the gaaf giraffe look is really in. |
| \<Loren\> | Oui! In Paris all the designers are trying for the gaaf giraffe look. Très chic! |
| \<Deeder\> | You guys stink. I like my bandanna! |
| \<Loren\> | And we like you, too, Deeder. Don't take it personally. |
| \<Deeder\> | Yeah. Like you're the one to talk. |
| \<Loren\> | Ah, now it is my turn. |
| \<Deeder\> | You bet it is! Monsieur Frenchman-with-a-Beret! |
| \<Loren\> | I like my beret. It is a symbol of my country. |
| \<Deeder\> | And a symbol to everyone else that you're a nerd. |
| \<Josh\> | A bald nerd! |
| \<Loren\> | I'm not bald! |
| \<Josh\> | Yeah, but your hair is so short the beret covers up most of it. |
| \<Tereza\> | It is short, Loren. What happened to you? |
| \<Loren\> | It is my sister's fault. She is in school for hair styling and wanted to cut my hair. I said yes and it was a big mistake. |

```
<Sanjeev>   that's for sure. the razor slip or
            something?
<Loren>     No! She says this is a very fashionable
            style.
<Tereza>    Probably goes well with the gaaf giraffe
            look, huh?
<Loren>     You are all terrible.
<Tereza>    We are. But, all together now:
<Deeder>    We
<Tereza>    love
<Josh>      you
<Sanjeev>   dude!
<Loren>     Well, now you have had your fun with me.
            What about Becky?

  . . .

  . . .
<Loren>     Someone must have something to say . . .
            Deeder?

  . . .

  . . .
<Deeder>    Can't think of a thing. I was surprised by
            Becky's picture.
<Becky>     Why do you say that?
<Deeder>    To be honest, I didn't think you'd be
            blond. Those pictures make you look like a
            model.
<Tereza>    You are very beautiful, Becky. Brains and
            beauty together! You must get a lot of
            attention at school.
<Becky>     Uhh . . . kinda. Thanks.
<Tereza>    It's great seeing what everyone looks like.
            You all mean very much to me. But I've got
            to study now. Is there anything else?
<Sanjeev>   yeah. i have something.
<Tereza>    Go ahead, Sanjeev.
```

```
<Sanjeev>  what did everyone think of my latest curry
           recipe?
  . . .
  . . .
<Sanjeev>  i thought so! these aren't some recipes i
           cut out of a magazine! i work hard on them.
           that last one is based on my great-
           grandmother's vindaloo.
<Josh>     But it sounds so weird, Sanj. I've never
           had this kind of food. It's totally
           different from McDonalds.
<Sanjeev>  mcdonalds?! you're getting close to
           insulting, josh.
<Deeder>   I've had Indonesian curry many times. It
           can't be that different.
<Sanjeev>  indonesian curry? you can't compare my
           curry to indonesian curry!
<Tereza>   I've been really busy, Sanjeev. I'm sorry.
           It takes a lot of effort to cook food that's
           totally new.
<Sanjeev>  you don't understand. this isn't just food.
           this is *art*.
<Loren>    All right, Sanjeev. I will try to make the
           recipe soon.
<Deeder>   Yeah.
<Sanjeev>  all right.
<Tereza>   We're done. Talk to everyone soon. Bye.
<Becky>    Bye.
<Sanj>     oujo
<Deeder>   Daag.
<Loren>    Bye.
<Josh>     See ya.


[TEREZA HAS LOGGED OFF]
[BECKY HAS LOGGED OFF]
```

```
[SANJEEV HAS LOGGED OFF]
[DEEDER HAS LOGGED OFF]
[LOREN HAS LOGGED OFF]
[JOSH HAS LOGGED OFF]

COMM TRANSCRIPT COMPLETE
CYBER.KDZ COMMBOT TERMINATING EXECUTION
TIME: 17:31 GMT
```

# [11]

The next Saturday, as she stood beneath the school office windows, Becky was surprised at how unafraid she was.

*Maybe I'm getting too used to this*, she thought.

That made her smile. When she had sneaked into Eastern SecureTech a few months before, it had been to stop some terrorists. And she'd ended up saving Deeder's life. When she'd gotten into the school office last week, it was because Loren was so sure someone had tampered with the grades database. Now she was going to set up a trap to catch that person. These were hardly the actions of a hardened criminal.

*But I'm not sure Loren and Deeder are right*, she thought. *I don't even know if someone really changed my grade. I could be going through all this for nothing.*

The window of the principal's office was about four feet off the ground. Becky had a tough time pulling herself up and in. She got stuck halfway and for a few moments her kicking legs were clearly visible above the top of the hedges. But it was the weekend and the school was deserted. Luckily, no one saw her.

Finally she grabbed the edge of the radiator with her fingertips. That gave her the extra pull she needed to slide into the office. She rolled onto the floor, stopped for a moment, and listened. There wasn't a sound.

She got up and crept to the outer office. Everything was as it had been last week. The computer sat silently in the corner. This time she noticed a tall philodendron in a pot next to the computer desk

*Great!* Becky thought. *That's the perfect spot.*

She'd been worried about finding a place to hide the video camera. The camera wasn't that big, but as Deeder had said in his last email, she couldn't just tape it to the top of the monitor. She had to make sure it and its cable were well hidden.

Becky swung her backpack off and pulled out the camera, a cable, and a diskette. She set them on the desk, leaned over, and carefully pulled the computer away from the wall. Deeder had sent her exact instructions on what to do. First she popped the diskette in the drive and hit the power switch. The computer hummed. As it booted off the diskette, Sanj's install program automatically kicked in. It copied some files to hidden directories, then searched the computer hardware for the modem. Once it had been found, it did a modem test and then began searching for a free serial port. Becky was impressed with how well Deeder and Sanj's program worked.

*Those guys are so smart,* she thought. *No one knows this stuff like they do. What a great team to be a part of.*

The computer beeped. A message flashed on the screen:
—>>> CYBER.KDZ SPYCAM <<<—
HEY AGENT STRAHN! TRY SERIAL PORT 2 . . .
PRESS <ENTER> TO CONTINUE

Becky laughed. She grabbed the cable and plugged one end into the camera. She looked at the back of the computer, found port 2, and plugged in the other end. Then she hit <Enter>.

The disk drive whirred and Becky waited as the screen message changed to:

SEARCHING FOR CAMERA . . .

After a few moments the message changed again:

HEY, AGENT STRAHN. I CAN'T FIND THE CAMERA. EITHER YOU PLUGGED IT INTO THE WRONG PORT OR WE'VE GOT A BIG PROBLEM. PRESS <ENTER> TO CONTINUE.

Becky's heart skipped a beat. She jumped and spun around as she heard a noise behind her. It was the telephone answering machine again. She took a deep breath to calm herself and reread the message. She looked behind the computer and checked the port the camera was plugged into. It was the right one. She jiggled the cable to make sure it was set correctly.

She slumped back down in her seat. What was wrong? She pressed the <Enter> key. The message changed:

ONE MORE THING. YOU MIGHT WANT TO CHECK THE CAMERA. DID YOU PLUG IT IN? HELLO? YOU KNOW, POWER? PRESS <ENTER> TO CONTINUE

Becky looked down at the camera lying on the table. Power! Deeder was a kook—but a smart kook. She pulled the power supply out of her backpack and plugged one end into a wall socket and the other end into the camera. She flipped up the power switch on the back of the camera then hit <Enter> on the keyboard.

The error message didn't go away.

She looked at the camera. The power switch was off. She flipped it on and hit <Enter> again. Nothing. She picked up the camera. The switch was off. She toggled it on and watched it spring back to the off position. The switch was defective.

*I'll need something to keep the switch on*, Becky thought. *A rubber band will be perfect.*

There was a plastic container on the desk filled with paper clips and rubber bands. She picked one out and tried to attach it to the back of the camera.

*This is way too big*, Becky said to herself. *I need a really small one.*

She sorted through the container and picked out the smallest bands she could find. But each one was too big.

"Darn!" she said, and plopped down in the chair in front of the computer. "What am I going to do now?"

Becky looked around the office, hoping for an idea. Even in the dim light it wasn't hard to spot what she needed. Lying on the desk, at the base of the computer, was a tiny fluorescent red rubber band. It was only about a half inch long. It was perfect. She hooked one end over the power switch and the other end to a screw that held the back of the camera on. Then she hit <Enter> again.

The diskette whirred. This time no message appeared. Instead, she was looking at a sideways shot of her arm. The camera was working.

She picked the camera up and slowly scanned the room while watching the monitor. Though it was dark, she could clearly make out the desks, the windows, everything. She hit <Enter> again.

GOOD JOB, AGENT STRAHN. SOFTWARE AND CAMERA ARE SUCCESSFULLY INSTALLED. NOW HIDE THE CAMERA. WHEN YOU ARE FINISHED, YOU MUST DESTROY ALL EVIDENCE THAT YOU WERE HERE. THAT MEANS YOU HAVE TO EAT THE DISKETTE.

(POWER DOWN WHEN CAMERA IS MOUNTED)

Becky laughed. She got up and placed the camera among the leaves of the potted plant. Then she sat back down and looked at the shot. It was a perfect image of her shoulder. She continued adjusting the camera and checking the shot until it looked right. She pulled some long pieces of twine out of her pack and tied the camera in place. Then she ran the power cord down along the stalk of the plant and behind the pot to the socket.

When everything was set, Becky popped the diskette out of the drive, powered down the computer, and grabbed her pack. She made sure nothing looked out of place.

*Pretty good job, if you ask me,* she said to herself, as she walked into the principal's office. She held the blind up so she could crawl out the window. She dropped to the ground and then closed the window tightly. Then she worked her way through the shrubs to the other side of the building, close to the sidewalk. Just as she was about to step out from behind the bushes, she froze. She heard voices. Two people were just on the other side of the shrubbery.

"He is *too* the cutest boy on the football team. I don't care *what* you say."

"No way," said Melissa. "Chuck Blakey is."

Becky recognized the voices. It was Jenny Sloat and Melissa Marek.

"Chuck's real cute but I want Dean. *Dean the Dream.*"

The way Jenny said it made Becky feel a little ill. She peeked through the branches. The two girls were standing a few feet away, holding several bags. Becky figured they must be coming home from shopping.

"Well, it doesn't matter, anyway." Melissa said. "They'll never notice us as long as we're freshmen and they're juniors."

"That's what you say. I'm going to get Dean's attention."

"How are you going to do that?"

"How do you think? Cheerleading! I'm going to be, like, the best cheerleader on the squad. Then he'll notice me."

"But what about your grades?"

"Oh, that . . . ? Like, no problem. I got an A in history so Mom's totally on my side now. She told Dad that if I was getting such good grades I could do any extra activities I wanted."

Becky felt awful now. *An A in history?* How could she have done that?

"You're kidding! That's great, Jenny! Especially since you blew your presentation. You must have done a lot of extra work."

"For sure. But it doesn't matter what I have to do, as long as I get on the squad. Hey, I gotta go home. I have to help my brother water and weed the roof garden."

"I thought you hated your brother. Why are you helping him?"

"He did me a favor. I gotta go. See you Monday!"

"Yeah! 'Bye!"

The two girls walked off in opposite directions. Becky waited a while and then crawled out from behind the bushes.

*How did Jenny Sloat get an A when Mr. O failed me?* she thought, as she walked home. Becky had felt betrayed by Mr. O when she had gotten the F, but knowing he gave Jenny an A made him into a real Benedict Arnold. It also made her pretty sure that her F was for real. It was clear that Mr. O *did* have different standards for the students in his class.

*If he holds me to a higher standard,* she thought, *he must* really *have a low standard for her.*

# [12]

When Becky got home she found Paul sitting at their computer.

"Hey, twitch-head!"

"Pixel-pig!"

Paul jumped up. Becky grabbed him and gave him a hug.

"I missed you, Paulie."

"I missed you, too. At least, when I stopped to think about it."

"Did you have a good time?"

"You bet! It was totally cool. There were at least seven zillion different games to play. And we had competitions every day. I won three days in a row! The counselors called me 'Paul the Squall' 'cause my scores blew everyone else's away!"

"I'm glad you had fun."

"I did. I didn't want to come home."

"I can't believe I'm saying this, but I'm really happy you're back. I need a friendly face around here. It's been kind of crazy—you probably saw some of the emails. Last week was the worst, though—the day you left—that's when I got my report card." Becky lowered her voice to a whisper. "Did you read how I snuck into school and copied the grades database? That part was great. I've been thinking about becoming a corporate spy."

While Becky spoke, Paul sat back down in front of the computer. He looked at what he had been typing. Then he turned toward Becky. He wasn't smiling anymore.

Becky noticed immediately.

"What's the matter, Paulie?"

Paul glared at her. His lips and jaw were set tight.

"I was so happy to see you, I forgot how mad I am!"

"Mad? What did *I* do?"

"Like you don't know! When I asked the Kids last month if Jimmy could join Cyber.kdz, everyone said no. And you said no the loudest."

"Well, Jimmy's just some kid you know from the video arcade. That doesn't get him into Cyber.kdz."

"He's not just *some kid*. He's almost as good as I am at Devastation Derby. And he's my friend."

"So what? Just 'cause someone's your friend doesn't get them into Cyber.kdz, either—you know that."

"That's what everyone said to me last month. But it's a good enough reason to let Kim in! She hardly even knows what a computer is but you get her in 'cause she's your friend! That stinks!"

Becky stared at Paul. He glared back.

"What are you talking about, Paulie? Kim's not in Cyber.kdz."

"Don't lie, dork-brain. I saw her picture in the yearbook . . ."

Slowly a smile began to spread across Becky's face. Seeing that made Paul even more angry.

"It's not funny, moron."

Becky got a grip on herself. "I'm sorry, Paul. It's just

I forgot about that. Kim's not in Cyber.kdz. Honest. That picture's not of her . . . it's of me.''

"What? It's not you. I know what Kim looks like.''

"No. It is Kim, but it's me on the Net.''

Paul looked really confused.

"What are talking about . . . ?''

Becky pulled a chair over and sat down.

"When you left, I decided there was no way I was putting pictures of me on CKServer.''

"Yeah, I know.''

"But I didn't know what I was going to do. Unfortunately, when I was uploading your images Loren was working on CKServer and he made me promise to put something up right away so he could finish the yearbook.''

"And you promised?''

"Yeah. Anyway, Kim had come over that afternoon and we were playing around with the video. You know how she is about having her picture taken.''

Paul rolled his eyes. Becky continued.

"So I had all these great images of Kim and I put those up there instead.''

"You mean the Kids think you look like Kim?''

"Yeah, that's it.'' Becky's smiled faded away.

"Beck . . . that's not right.''

Becky looked down. Paul continued.

"The Kids love *you*. They won't care.''

"Yes, they will!'' Becky snapped back. "You promised you wouldn't say anything!''

"Cool it, Beck. I won't say anything.'' Paul looked up at the computer screen. "But it may be too late . . .'' He nodded toward the monitor.

Becky leaned forward to read the message. It was a tirade of the kind only Paul could do. He accused the Kids of liking Becky more than him because they let her friend Kim into Cyber.kdz when they wouldn't let Jimmy in. He used about every insult he knew and ended by saying that he was quitting unless Kim was thrown out of Cyber.kdz tomorrow.

Becky's face went pale as she read the email.

"P-P-Paul, did you send this?!"

Paul looked down at his shoes. "I'm sorry, Beck. I didn't know. If you'd only come home a few minutes earlier, you could have stopped me."

Becky dropped her head in her hands. "No! I can't believe this! No! Please say it's not true, Paulie. Please . . . !"

Paul smiled. "Okay. It's not true."

Becky looked up. *"What?"*

"You said to say it's not true, so I did."

"But is it?"

"Is it what?"

"Not true!"

"I said it was, didn't I?"

Becky looked mad. "Paul, tell me right now. Did you send that email or not? You won't be able to move your arm for a week if you don't." She raised her fist menacingly.

Paul grabbed the mouse. "Don't hit me! You touch me and I'll click 'send'! I will!"

Becky broke into a big smile. "Then you didn't send it! You scared me, you jerk."

"Better not call me names. I've still got the pointer over 'send' . . ."

"Please delete it, Paul. Please . . ."

"Hmmm . . . let's see. What are you gonna give me?"

"What do you want?"

94

"StarStreak portable VR helmet."

"I don't even know what that is, but it sounds expensive."

"And you can take my turn doing the dishes for a month."

"You're crazy!"

"All right . . ." Paul clicked the mouse.

*"Paul!"*

"Just kidding. Look."

Becky leaned toward the screen. The message was gone and the mouse pointer was over the delete button.

"Thanks, Paulie."

"You really thought I'd be so mean?"

"Uh, no."

"But it's not over, Becky."

"What do you mean?"

"You can't fool the Kids forever. Something's gonna happen someday and they'll find out. They won't like it. They won't trust you if you don't tell them before they find out on their own."

"They won't find out."

"That's what you say. But if Cyber.kdz can catch terrorists, they can find out that you put your friend's picture on the Net instead of your own."

# [13]

COMM TRANSCRIPT
COLLECTED BY CYBER.KDZ COMMBOT
TIME: 18:00 GMT (SATURDAY)
ONLINE:    TEREZA
           LOREN
           BECKY
           PAUL
           JOSH
BEGIN TRANSCRIPT. . . . .

<Paul>      Hey, where's Sanj and Deeder?
<Tereza>    Hello, Paul. It's nice to have you back.
<Loren>     Bonsoir, everyone. I think that is a hint,
            Paul.
<Paul>      A hint about what?
<Loren>     You did not even say hello.
<Paul>      Oh that. Hi. Now, where's Sanj and Deeder?
<Becky>     Hi, everyone. Please excuse the twerp.
<Tereza>    What a pleasant greeting, Paul. To answer
            your question, Sanjeev is visiting
            relatives. He'll be logging on late. Deeder
            had to help his aunt move to a new
            apartment.
<Paul>      That stinks! I've been waiting all week to
            comm with them. I wanted to let them know

96

about the Air Destruction prototype I
started at camp.

&lt;Josh&gt;     How was camp?

&lt;Paul&gt;     So cool you wouldn't even believe it. But I
can't get Air Destruction to work. It's
really hard. I need the wizards to help me.

&lt;Josh&gt;     Maybe we can do it as a Cyber.kdz project
now that the yearbook is done.

&lt;Tereza&gt;     That's something we can talk about. It
depends on whether Sanj has the time.

&lt;Paul&gt;     Sure, he'll have the time. This is the most
perfect game ever!

&lt;Tereza&gt;     We'll see. In the meantime, we have to
figure out what's going on with the spy-cam.

&lt;Becky&gt;     I haven't checked lately. Any pictures?

&lt;Loren&gt;     Not a single image. Perhaps no one is
accessing the database.

&lt;Josh&gt;     Or something is wrong with the transmission
protocol Sanj and Deeder wrote.

&lt;Loren&gt;     I do not think so. As Paul says, they are
wizards.

&lt;Tereza&gt;     What could be wrong, then?

&lt;Josh&gt;     Maybe whoever changed the grades isn't
interested in causing any more problems.

&lt;Becky&gt;     Or maybe there wasn't anyone in the first
place.

&lt;Loren&gt;     You may be right, Becky. But you may be
wrong. Deeder and I have enough experience
chasing scum to know that they do not get
bored easily. When scum find a way to make
trouble, they can not stay away from it.
This person will be back. Trust me. C'est
vrai. It is true.

&lt;Josh&gt;     I think Loren's right.

&lt;Paul&gt;     So do I.

&lt;Becky&gt;     Then why aren't we catching him?

| | |
|---|---|
| \<Tereza\> | Or her. |
| \<Becky\> | Yeah. Or her. That reminds me . . . when I sent that email about setting up the camera, I forgot to tell you something else that happened. When I was sneaking away from the school, I overheard Jenny Sloat talking to Melissa Marek about her grades. Jenny said she got an A in history. |
| \<Josh\> | So what's the big deal? |
| \<Becky\> | The big deal is that Jenny's terrible at history. She failed almost every test. And she was all panicky because if she failed the class her parents wouldn't let her be a cheerleader. |
| \<Loren\> | This is good information. If she needed a good grade in history, then perhaps she is the one who changed the grades. |
| \<Becky\> | I don't think that's possible. Jenny has trouble just turning on a computer. In computer lab she's always running to the teacher to help her with the easiest things. I don't see how she could figure out how to get into the grades database and change things around. |
| \<Paul\> | Beck's right. One of her brothers is in my class and I went to a birthday party at his house. Jenny's dumb. Her parents bought her a VCR for her birthday and she couldn't figure out how to set the clock. We told her that when the time flashed 12:00 it meant that the VCR might explode. She believed us and ran out of the room! It was great! |
| \<Josh\> | You're so mean, Paul. But that's pretty funny. |
| \<Loren\> | I still think it may be important. But we |

|  |  |
|---|---|
| | need to find out why the images have not transferred. |
| <Becky> | Loren, do you know how Deeder set the program to connect to the wire? |
| <Loren> | He had a local New York telephone number. You know how he has these lists of mysterious numbers. He wanted to use a local one so your school wouldn't be charged for a long-distance call. |
| <Becky> | Did he put a 9 in front of the number? |
| <Loren> | I don't know. Why? |
| <Becky> | Because you have to dial a 9 to get an outside line from inside the school. If it doesn't dial a 9 first, the spy-cam program will never connect to the wire. |
| <Tereza> | I think you've got it, Becky. How could Deeder know that? |
| <Josh> | There could be lots of images sitting on the hard disk right now. One of them could be the scum who changed the grade. |
| <Loren> | I hope there are not lots of images. If there are too many, the hard disk will run out of space and the system will crash. Then the spy-cam will be discovered. |
| <Paul> | Yeah. And we need to get the camera back for Air Destruction. I think we will need two cameras for each player. |
| <Becky> | That doesn't matter now, Paul! We can't have the school computer crash! We have to change that phone number. |
| <Josh> | Agent Strahn called to duty again! |
| <Tereza> | How are you going to do it this time, Becky? |
| <Becky> | I don't know. It will be harder now 'cause school's back in session. I'll just scout it out and see what happens. |

```
<Paul>     I'll do it! I can sneak in wearing my
           StarStreak VR helmet.
<Josh>     Where'd you get that? Those things cost
           about 200 bucks!
<Paul>     I don't have it yet. Becky's gonna buy it
           for me.
<Josh>     You're kidding?! That's great. Buy me one
           too, Beck!
<Becky>    He's kidding, Josh. I don't have $200.
<Paul>     I thought we had a deal . . .
<Josh>     What deal?
<Becky>    Nothing. Now shut up, Paul. Hey Loren, will
           you update Deeder on all this and have him
           send me instructions on changing the phone
           number?
<Loren>    Oui. I will do it.
[SANJEEV HAS JOINED THE COMM]
<Sanjeev>  hey kids, sorry i'm late. what did i miss?
<Tereza>   Hi, Sanjeev. We're almost done. I'll send
           you an update by email.
<Paul>     Wait! We're not done. I have to talk to you,
           Sanj! I started Air Destruction at camp.
           All the counselors said it was a great
           idea. But it's really hard. You gotta help
           me!
<Sanjeev>  hey, paul-dude. stay cool. if the kids want
           to do it, we'll make it happen. but i got a
           lot of schoolwork right now.
<Paul>     The yearbook's done, Sanj. PLEASE! I'll do
           anything!
<Sanjeev>  yeah?
<Paul>     Yeah.
<Sanjeev>  all right. for every day i work on it, you
           have to make one of my curry recipes.
<Paul>     YECCHH!
<Becky>    Paul! That's so rude.
```

```
<Sanjeev>  don't do it, then. i don't think i'll have
           any free time for another year or three.
<Paul>     NO! Come on! I told you before that I can't
           eat that weird stuff. It's not cereal.
<Sanjeev>  if that's how you want it . . .
<Josh>     You guys are really funny to listen to . . .
<Paul>     Shut up, space-case.
<Becky>    Don't tease Paul, Josh.
<Tereza>   I thought this comm was about over . . .
<Paul>     Wait! Sanj, you'll do it if I make that
           curry stuff?
<Sanjeev>  yeah
<Paul>     I'll do that. No prob. Start programming
           tomorrow, OK?
<Sanjeev>  you're not gonna get out of it that easy,
           paul. when i say make, i mean make and eat.
<Paul>     Shoot!
<Loren>    Sanj has given you an offer Paul. You have
           to decide.
<Paul>     OK. I'll do it.
<Sanjeev>  cool dude. you start cooking the curry and
           i'll cook the code. becky will make sure
           you keep your end of the bargain.
<Becky>    You bet I will.
<Tereza>   All right. I think we're done now. Good
           luck, Becky. Email us when you've fixed the
           spy-cam.
<Becky>    I will. So long.
<Tereza>   Adeus.
<Sanjeev>  see ya.
<Josh>     Bye. Enjoy your meal, Paul!
<Paul>     Go eat some green cheese, moon-brain.
<Loren>    Bon appetite, Paul. Au revoir.
[BECKY HAS LOGGED OFF]
[TEREZA HAS LOGGED OFF]
[SANJEEV HAS LOGGED OFF]
```

```
[JOSH HAS LOGGED OFF]
[PAUL HAS LOGGED OFF]
[LOREN HAS LOGGED OFF]
COMM TRANSCRIPT COMPLETE
CYBER.KDZ COMMBOT TERMINATING EXECUTION
TIME: 18:19 GMT
```

# [14]

From: **Deeder**, rodan@netherspace.nl
To: **Becky**, historian@nyc.net.us
Date: Mon, 07:28 (Mon, 06:28 GMT)
Subject: Number 9, Number 9, Number 9

Hey Beck-babe,
Got the word from Loren that I forgot a little something. I've never made any phone calls from your school—how was I supposed to know?
But we'll get this handled. It's an easy fix. Here's what you need to do.
From the DOS prompt type SPYCAM and press <Enter>. Then hold down the <Alt> key immediately. That's a little security check to make sure people don't start the program by accident. You'll see a welcome screen (a Deed-man and Sanj special!) and then press <Ctrl> P. A box will pop up with the phone number in it. Add a 9 and a comma before the number (the comma tells the program to pause for a second while it waits for the outside line).
That's it. The graphics should upload as soon as it can connect.
Good luck, Agent Strahn. Have fun. Whooo-eee!

Deed

P.S. Sanj told me about his deal with your brother. Tell Paul I hope he's hungry!

Becky printed the email, folded it, and put it in her coat pocket. She grabbed her books and headed for the front door.

"Aren't you having breakfast, dear?" her mom called from the kitchen.

"No, Mom. I have a special project I need to do before my first class."

"Skipping breakfast isn't healthy, Becky," her mom replied.

Becky suppressed a laugh as she stuck her head in the kitchen. Her mom was leaning against the counter, her briefcase in one hand and a breakfast bar in the other.

"I'll survive, Mom. 'Bye, Dad. 'Bye, Paulie."

Paul didn't look up from the cereal box he was reading. Her dad mumbled something and turned the page of his history book.

"Make sure you eat a healthy lunch!" Mrs. Strahn called after her.

Becky arrived at school about twenty-five minutes before the first bell. She'd never been to school this early and wasn't even sure the office would be open.

She was surprised to find that not only was it open, but it was very busy as well. Secretaries, administrators, and teachers filled the place, talking on phones, shuffling files, and filling out forms. A large woman was sitting at the computer with her back toward Becky. Her head bobbed up and down as she pounded the keys.

*Shoot*, Becky thought, *this won't work. There's way too much going on.*

She looked over toward the philodendron in the corner. She thought she could just glimpse a tiny reflection from the camera lens hidden in the leaves.

*"Dolores! Dolores! It's doing it again!"*

Becky saw the woman sitting at the computer raise her hands above her head and shake them. She turned toward one of the other administrators.

"This computer's gone crazy, Dolores! I'm telling you, it doesn't like me. It hates me! And *I* hate *it!*"

"That's the problem, Steph," Dolores replied. "It knows you hate it, so it doesn't treat you right. You can't go saying mean things to these computers—they have chips in 'em that sense when they're being mistreated, and those chips make 'em misbehave. It's called artificial intelligence."

"It can be artificial stupidity, for all I care!" Steph shouted. "I just want to get my work done and this thing keeps beeping at me when it shouldn't, telling me it's run out of space or something. How can that be? There's plenty of room here. I've moved everything off the desk. I'm not even putting my coffee cup near it. How can it be running out of space!"

Becky watched as Steph pushed herself away from the computer desk with a great "harrumph," stood up, and walked out of the office.

"I'm taking a break or I'll go mad!"

Steph stormed right past Becky and strode out the front door. Becky looked back at the computer, now sitting there unused. There was still no way she could get to it; the rest of the office was full of people. She turned and followed Steph outside.

Steph was sitting on a bench a few yards from the front door. Her eyes were shut and frustration showed in the creases around her tightly closed mouth.

"Oh, Lord," Steph muttered, "why do you torment me with that ridiculous machine? Please help me. I've just got to get my work done today . . ."

Becky walked over and sat down. As she did, she let out a sigh. Steph looked up.

"What's the matter with you?" she asked, not too kindly.

"Oh, nothing . . ." Becky sighed in her best "I really mean everything" voice.

Steph smiled, glad to forget her own troubles for a minute.

"C'mon, darling. Steph can tell when someone's feeling blue . . ."

"Well, my alarm clock got all messed up and I woke up an hour early and ended up at school a half-hour before class."

"That doesn't seem so bad. Why are you worrying your head about that?"

"It's just that I really needed the sleep. I was up all night trying to fix my computer. I kept getting a message that I was 'out of space' and I knew I *couldn't* be. It was driving me crazy!"

Becky watched Steph's eyes light up with interest. She continued.

"I couldn't go to bed until I solved the problem. I finally did, but it was three A.M. And I didn't get my homework done, either."

Steph leaned across the bench toward Becky.

"Out of space? That's wonderful! I mean, that's terrible! You fixed it. *You* fixed it?"

Becky nodded.

Steph grabbed Becky's face between her hands and squeezed.

"You're an angel, sent from heaven to help me!"

Becky tried hard to sound innocent.

"What are you talking about?"

"You! You, darling! You're gonna save my life. I have a computer that's doing the same thing to me that yours did to you, and it's driving me mad! If you can fix yours, then you can fix mine!"

Steph jumped up, grabbed Becky by the hand, and yanked her off the bench.

"C'mon . . . what's your name, dear?"

"Becky Strahn."

"C'mon, Becky. My angel of mercy!"

Steph towed Becky up the stairs and through the front doors. The hall was more crowded now as students arrived for class. Steph plowed a path through them and into the office.

"Dolores! Dolores! Look what I found. My troubles are over!"

Dolores didn't look up from her desk. "What are you going on about now, Steph?"

"I found an angel, an angel sent to relieve me from my suffering."

Steph pulled Becky through the maze of desks and back to the computer. She grabbed her by the shoulders and pushed her down into the chair.

"You sit right here and do your magic, honey. Whatever you did to your computer, just repeat it."

Becky looked up into Steph's hopeful face.

"I'll try. I don't know if I can fix it, but I'll try."

She turned back to the monitor. Steph stood watching

Becky's fingers click the keys and the characters appear and disappear on the monitor.

*I can't change the phone number with her looking over my shoulder like this,* Becky thought. *I'll have to figure out a way to get rid of her.*

While she thought, she entered some standard DOS commands, like DIR, MEM, and EDIT, so Steph would think she was working.

Five minutes passed. Steph didn't move.

"Are you getting it?" Steph asked eagerly. "Does it have something to do with that artificial intelligence microchip? If I'd have known about that I wouldn't have called it all those bad names . . ."

"This is tricky," Becky said. "But I think I'm getting close."

What seemed like another five minutes went by. Becky had displayed the directory structure about twenty times. Steph was still standing at her elbow. She'd catch on soon and figure out that Becky wasn't really doing anything.

Finally the bell for first period rang through the office. Becky looked up at the clock, then at Steph.

"I'm late for class," she said.

"Now, don't you worry about that. You're not moving until you fix this computer. Tell me who your teacher is, and I'll go myself and say you're doing a special project to save the school."

"I have geometry with Ms. Alexander."

"All right. You just keep working. I'll let her know. I've got to drop off these order forms with the custodian, so I'll be back in five minutes. Don't you stop, now."

Steph turned on her heel and headed out the door. Becky looked around. The office was less crowded now.

The teachers were all in class, and many of the administrators were running errands around campus. Only three secretaries were left, along with the principal, in her office. Becky reached into her pocket and pulled out Deeder's email. She quickly followed the instructions and started the spy-cam program. The welcome screen appeared. Kim was staring out from the monitor at Becky.

"What is Kim doing in this program?" Becky wondered. Then she looked at the caption below the picture.

SpyCam
written exclusively for
Agent Strahn [alias Becky]
by
the Wizards of the Wire
sanj and the Deed-Man

Seeing her name under Kim's picture explained it. Sanj and Deeder had copied one of the pictures Becky had uploaded for the Cyber.kdz Yearbook. She had forgotten that they thought she looked like Kim.

Quickly she hit <Ctrl> P and a box popped up with the phone number in it. She inserted a 9 and a comma, saved the changes, and closed the program.

She looked around. No one had noticed a thing. It had taken less than a minute to make the change. She leaned over and glanced at the modem sitting behind the computer. She saw the lights flicker as the spy-cam program dialed. When she saw the carrier detect light go on, she knew it had connected to the modem on the other end of the line. Then the transmit and receive

lights began flashing. The images were being transferred!

Becky looked back at the screen. The main menu was
displayed. She followed the choices down to the
GRADES DATABASE option. The image of the F in the
middle of her report card appeared in her mind. Then
she thought about Jenny Sloat bragging about her A.
Could she really have gotten an A? Maybe she'd been
lying to impress Melissa.

Becky looked at the clock. She had at least two or
three minutes before Steph returned. She looked around
at the other secretaries. They were all busy typing or
talking on the phone. Becky keyed down and hit
<Enter>.

The grades program started. Becky quickly selected
the search screen and typed SLOAT, JENNY. A list of
classes appeared. Becky scanned the row of letters to
the right of each class. One B, a lot of C's, and an A.
An A in history! Staring at that A made Becky really
angry! She hit <Esc>.

"Becky! Becky! How are you *doing?*"

Becky hit <Esc> a second time and then quickly selected EXIT. The screen returned to the main menu just
as Steph appeared at Becky's side.

"Did you get it?"

Becky stood up. "Yes. I think it's all fixed. You
won't have any more trouble."

"A saint! An angel! An answer to my prayers!"

Steph grabbed Becky and gave her a great bear hug.

"Thanks, dear!" she continued. "I owe you one."
She leaned closer and whispered, "If you ever have an
unexcused absence . . . you just see me, okay, sweetie?"

"Sure, thanks. I should really get to class now."

"All right. You do that. And remember what I said."

Becky grabbed her books and headed out of the office. As she walked into the hall, she could still hear Steph bellowing behind her.

"Dolores! That girl's a genius. An angel *and* a genius. I knew it when she sat down next to me. Sent from heaven to end my troubles . . ."

Steph sat down at her computer and started her work. She wasn't getting the mysterious out-of-space message anymore. But the computer seemed a bit slow.

She didn't know that the computer was pretty busy with a lot of background processing: there was a week's worth of large graphic files to transfer across the Net. One by one it compressed the images and sent them through the wire to CKServer. Finally there was only one image left: an image that the spy-cam program had captured only a few minutes before. It compressed it and transferred the file. Then it hung up. The files were now safely stored on CKServer, waiting to be viewed by the Kids. Including that last file: an image of Becky Strahn.

# [15]

Becky was feeling pretty good about things as she walked home from school on Wednesday. The Kids were having a comm this evening to review the images uploaded by the spy-cam program. Deeder had done a quick check on them and had emailed everyone saying that there was an excellent possibility for apprehending the culprit. Maybe she was wrong and someone *had* changed her grade. Besides that, Brad Sloat hadn't bugged her all week and she'd aced the day's pop quiz in history. It was definitely one of the better days she'd had.

At home, the aroma of curry filled the apartment. Her dad was sitting at the kitchen table with his nose in a book. Paul stood at the counter, his arms covered in orange-brown powder. Little seeds coated his hair. Bowls, dishes, and spoons were scattered everywhere. Paul did not look happy.

"Hmmm . . . very interesting . . ." Mr. Strahn said, and then continued reading aloud. " 'It is important to remember that curry is not a single spice, but rather a combination of spices. In India, curries have been made the traditional way for centuries. The cook begins by gathering a wealth of spices, then pounds them together and fries the mixture in hot oil to make a *tadka,* or curry paste.' ''

Paul noticed Becky standing in the doorway.

"What are you looking at?" he asked grumpily.

"Nothing. Just wondering how your project was going. Having a good time?"

Mr. Strahn looked up.

"Hello, Becky. Paul and I are cooking together. We're making Indian recipes that are hundreds of years old. It's great fun."

Paul groaned. Mr. Strahn continued.

"Did you know that the spice trade was responsible for the diverse nature of curries around the world? I had no idea it was such a fascinating subject. We're having a wonderful time. Why don't you join us?"

"Uh, that's okay, Dad. I have a lot of work to do. You two go ahead. I wouldn't want to get in the way of your fun." She backed out of the kitchen with Paul glaring at her.

In her room Becky called Kim and talked for a while, laughing about the noises that were coming out of the kitchen. Then she did her homework and read. Paul passed by her door a few minutes before the comm was set to start.

"Better clean up, twitch-head," Becky called from her bed. "Comm's gonna start soon, and you don't want to get that stuff all over the keyboard . . ."

A few minutes later he was back at her door.

"How'd it go?" Becky asked, sitting down at the computer.

Paul didn't look at her. "I don't want to talk about it," he said. "When's the comm?"

"In about three minutes. Isn't it fun to learn something new, instead of standing in front of a video game all day?"

Paul didn't answer. He dragged another chair to the computer and pulled the second keyboard closer.

"Well, isn't it?" Becky pressed.

"No, it's not!" Paul snapped. "Do you know what it feels like to get turmeric in your eye? It hurts! And these coriander seeds got in my hair and I can't get them out. Look at my fingers . . ." He held up his hands, which were stained a deep brownish-red. "They'll never be clean again. And I don't even like to eat this stuff . . ." His voice trailed off sadly.

"But Sanj is doing the programming for you, Paul. Don't forget that. You'll be happy when you can play Air Obstruction."

*"Destruction!"*

"Oh, yeah. But focus on that. It'll make you feel better."

"Why are you in such a good mood, pixel-pig?"

"I don't know. Things are going better at school. I aced my history quiz today. And Deeder thinks one of the spy-cam images is the scum who changed my grade. That is, if it wasn't Mr. O."

"Why don't you just *ask* Mr. O what he gave you, then you'll know for sure?"

"I would if I could. But Mr. O broke his leg hiking during vacation and won't be back for two more weeks."

"If the spy-cam did find the scum what are we gonna do to 'em?"

"I don't know yet. That's one of the things we're gonna comm about. Let's log on."

Paul quickly dialed in and they joined the comm.

```
COMM TRANSCRIPT
COLLECTED BY CYBER.KDZ COMMBOT
TIME: 23:00 GMT (WEDNESDAY)
ONLINE:    TEREZA
           DEEDER
           LOREN
           BECKY
           PAUL
           JOSH
           SANJEEV
BEGIN TRANSCRIPT. . . . .
```

| | |
|---|---|
| \<Tereza\> | Boa noite. |
| \<Becky\> | Hi everyone. |
| \<Josh\> | Hi. |
| \<Loren\> | Bonsoir. |
| \<Deeder\> | Hallo |
| \<Sanjeev\> | kemcho |
| \<Paul\> | Krigluz. |
| \<Deeder\> | What's Krigluz? |
| \<Paul\> | That's Galactarian for hello. If you are all going to speak a different language, then so can I. |
| \<Deeder\> | Where's Galactaria? |
| \<Paul\> | In my computer. It's the universe of Galactic Starfighter. Becky is the Galactic Empress and I'm the best starfighter in the universe. |
| \<Sanjeev\> | not surprised to hear that. |
| \<Deeder\> | You can't use Galactarian language during a comm, Paul. |
| \<Paul\> | Why not?! |
| \<Deeder\> | It's a Cyber.kdz rule. Only earth languages allowed online. |
| \<Paul\> | That's not fair! I bet if Josh wanted to speak some alien language you'd let him! |

| | |
|---|---|
| \<Deeder\> | Calm down, Paul. I was just kidding! It was a joke! Ha ha. Lighten up. |
| \<Paul\> | Funny, *Dead*man. |
| \<Becky\> | I'd go easy on him, Deeder. Paul's in kind of a bad mood tonight. |
| \<Paul\> | You'd be too if you had to spend all your time cooking and cleaning and eating orange goo . . . |
| \<Sanjeev\> | hey paul, you want out of the deal just say so. |
| \<Paul\> | NO! Keep coding. Don't stop! |
| \<Tereza\> | We have some really important things to cover. Let's move on. |
| \<Sanjeev\> | yeah, you're right. |
| \<Tereza\> | Go ahead, Deeder. |
| \<Deeder\> | Welcome, ladies and gentlemen, to the Amazing World of the Cyber.kdz spy-cam. Brought to you by Cyber.kdz! |
| \<Josh\> | Let's see 'em. |
| \<Deeder\> | All right. Everyone open a thread sled. Point it to CKServer/spy-cam. I wrote a percolator that will cycle through the pics at my command. |

. . .

. . .

| | |
|---|---|
| \<Deeder\> | Anyone NOT ready? |
| \<Becky\> | Just a second. Still loading. |

. . .

. . .

| | |
|---|---|
| \<Becky\> | All set. |
| \<Deeder\> | OK. There are 9 pics. Here's the first. |
| \<Becky\> | That's Dolores. She's one of the secretaries. |
| \<Deeder\> | Number 2. |
| \<Becky\> | And that's Steph. She works on the computer all the time. Nice lady. |

116

```
<Deeder>    Number 3.
<Becky>     I don't know who that is.
<Loren>     He looks like a STIK. I don't think the
            person who did this is an adult.
<Tereza>    I think Loren's right.
<Deeder>    Well if that's the case, we don't have to
            look at the next 5. They're all adults.
            Only the last one isn't.
<Tereza>    Why don't you go through them quickly
            anyway.
<Deeder>    All right. Number 4.
<Becky>     Don't know.
<Deeder>    Number 5.
<Becky>     That's the principal.
<Deeder>    Number 6.
<Becky>     Don't know.
<Deeder>    Number 7.
<Becky>     Vice-principal.
<Deeder>    Number 8.
<Becky>     I think that's one of the counselors.
<Deeder>    That only leaves number 9. This is the best
            candidate.
<Josh>      Let's see it.
<Deeder>    And the culprit is . . . number 9.
  . . .
  . . .
<Tereza>    Becky? Do you recognize her?
  . . .
  . . .
<Tereza>    Becky?
<Becky>     Uh, no. I don't know who it is.
<Paul>      Becky, that's
  . . .
  . . .
<Tereza>    Paul? What were you gonna say?
```

```
<Paul>     Nothing. I thought it was someone I know.
           But it's not.
<Sanjeev>  we found scum!
<Deeder>   Gotcha!
<Josh>     What do we do now?
<Loren>    I think we should put a copy of the database
           and this graphic on a diskette and send it
           to the principal immediately.
<Deeder>   Sounds perfect. I'll get the files together.
<Tereza>   Good job, Deeder, Sanj and, of course,
           Becky!
<Becky>    Wait a sec, Kids. I don't think this is who
           we're looking for.
<Deeder>   What are you talking about? Who else is it
           gonna be? Why would a student be on that
           computer accessing the grades database?
           And look at her expression. She looks
           worried or something.
<Josh>     Yeah. Kind of shifty. Like she's in a real
           hurry.
<Deeder>   This is the scum! Another KILL for
           Cyber.kdz! OOOOOEEEEEE!
<Becky>    Slow down, Deeder. I don't think this is
           the right person.
<Deeder>   You said that already. But why? Do you have
           a reason?
<Becky>    I just don't think so. I guess it's a
           feeling I have.
<Deeder>   WHAT?!! A feeling? Do you even *remember* the
           hard time you gave me when I had a *feeling*
           about those terrorist scum in New York?
<Tereza>   I don't understand, Becky. Why do you feel
           this way?
  . . .
  . . .
<Paul>     It's because of me. I told Becky that I
```

|           | think this is one of my friend's older |
|-----------|----------------------------------------|
|           | sisters. And she's a total goody-good. |
|           | There's no way she could do this.      |
| <Loren>   | Really? Are you sure?                   |
| <Becky>   | Paul's right. Why don't we hold off for a couple days and we can check it out. I want to make sure we do the right thing. |
| <Deeder>  | No way! We nailed this scum. Let's put her away. |
| <Becky>   | Just a couple days. All right? It would be terrible to get someone innocent in trouble. |
| <Tereza>  | If that's what you want to do, Becky, I'll go along with it. |
| <Josh>    | Me too.                                |
| <Loren>   | Et moi. And me.                        |
| <Sanjeev> | cool with me.                          |
| <Deeder>  | What's the matter with everyone? Getting soft with scum . . . this fails! |
| <Josh>    | It's only a few days, Deeder. It's not like this kid is going to leave town or anything. |
| <Deeder>  | All right. But just a couple of days. Until Friday. After that, the diskette gets sent. |
| <Tereza>  | Good. Let's meet on the beam again Friday night. 2300 GMT. See you then! |
| <Loren>   | Au revoir.                             |
| <Josh>    | Bye.                                   |
| <Deeder>  | Daag.                                  |
| <Sanjeev> | bye                                    |
| <Becky>   | Night.                                 |
| <Paul>    | Commander X is outta here.             |

[TEREZA HAS LOGGED OFF]
[LOREN HAS LOGGED OFF]
[JOSH HAS LOGGED OFF]
[DEEDER HAS LOGGED OFF]

```
[SANJEEV HAS LOGGED OFF]
[BECKY HAS LOGGED OFF]
[PAUL HAS LOGGED OFF]
COMM TRANSCRIPT COMPLETE
CYBER.KDZ COMMBOT TERMINATING EXECUTION
TIME: 23:14 GMT
```

## [16]

"How did your picture get on there?" Paul shouted, as soon as they were logged off.

"*Shhh,* quiet. Mom and Dad will hear you."

Paul lowered his voice. "Well, *how did it?*"

"I can't believe I was so stupid." Becky pushed her chair away from the desk. "After I fixed the spy-cam phone number, I took a peek at the grades database to see if Jenny Sloat really got an A in history. I didn't even think about the spy-cam taking my picture."

"That was so stupid!"

Becky turned toward her brother. "Thanks for covering for me. That was great, Paulie."

"Pretty quick, huh?"

"Yeah, but now I gotta do some fast thinking. I have to figure out who *really* changed the grades before Friday. Otherwise, the Kids are going to send *my* picture to the principal."

"That's not much time."

"You're telling me!"

Their discussion was cut short as Mrs. Strahn called them in to dinner.

"What's the matter with you?" Mrs. Strahn asked Becky, as they entered the kitchen. "Why the long face?"

"Oh, nothing, Mom," Becky answered. "Just some school stuff."

"Well, I'm sure you'll cheer up soon. Your father is so excited about helping Paul with his cooking project that we've decided to go out to dinner tonight."

"Burgerland?" Paul asked excitedly.

"Oh, no," answered Mr. Strahn. "I was sure you'd want to sample some other styles of curry. We're going out for Indian food."

The next day went by too quickly for Becky. Everybody she passed in the hall was a suspect. She wished she were a detective who could stop and question them. But there were hundreds of students flowing past her. They'd think she was crazy if she started grilling them. What was she going to do, shove them up against the lockers and force them to account for their whereabouts for the last three weeks?

In class Becky looked from desk to desk, sizing up each student. Jenny Sloat was the obvious suspect in history, but Paul was right about her: knowing as little about computers as she did, there was no way she could have changed Becky's grade. In P.E. she studied the other girls—especially the ones who had been so cruel throughout the year. But she couldn't imagine any of them sneaking into the school office to change computer records.

When she got home, Becky wanted desperately to call Kim. But she couldn't ask her for help. How could she explain about the spy-cam and the pictures on CKServer? Besides, she was sworn to secrecy about Cyber.kdz. Even if she could talk to Kim, it wouldn't do any good; Kim was a great friend, but she didn't think like a detective.

Paul came home from school and sat with her for a half hour. He thought he was helping, but his questions only irritated his sister. He escaped to the living room to play video games after Becky snapped at him for the third time.

"I still think it's important to know if anyone goes around your school wearing night-vision infrared goggles," he said as he left.

Becky lay back on her bed. *I need a detective,* she thought. *Someone like Sherlock Holmes, or Miss Marple.* Becky had read some Agatha Christie books a few years before. She never understood how Miss Marple could always figure out who'd done it.

*My mind just doesn't work that way,* she thought. But that got her to thinking about how her mind *did* work. She wasn't interested in crime—she was interested in history. And archaeology. *But archaeology is a lot like detective work* . . . she said to herself slowly. *You're only given part of the story and then you have to figure out what happened.*

Becky jumped up and grabbed a few books off her shelves. She laid them open on the bed and began poring over them: *Great Archaeological Finds*, *The Science of Archeology,* and *The Mystery of History.*

An hour later, Paul stuck his head in the door.

"In a better mood?" he asked.

Becky looked up. "Hey, Paulie. Did you know that the German archaeologist Heinrich Schliemann uncovered the ruins of Mycenae by following clues he found in ancient Greek plays?"

"What are you doing, Becky? You shouldn't be wasting time with that history stuff. You need to figure out who changed your grade before tomorrow night."

"I know. That's what I'm doing. I'm learning to be a detective."

Paul rolled his eyes. "You're learning to be a nut," he said. "And you're doing a good job at it." He walked away. Becky heard him scavenging through the cupboards in the kitchen.

It was 11:45 before Becky turned off the light and went to sleep. She had taken only a quick break for dinner and thirty minutes to power through her homework. She'd read everything she owned on how the minds of great archaeologists worked. Tomorrow she'd find out if she'd learned anything.

As she walked to her first class the next morning, Becky did feel as if she'd learned something. Her eye for detail was sharper. She noticed things she hadn't before . . . like the mail slot on the side of the school office.

*That may have been something the scum used*, she thought. *I don't know how, but it might be important.*

There was paint peeling from the wall next to the office door. It might have been scratched off when the scum broke in.

"Oink, oink!"

"Watch out, piggy!"

"Out of the way!"

The barbarians sped past her and disappeared around the corner at the end of hall. They were in such a rush that they didn't bother shoving her this time.

Time seemed to slow down for Becky during her first three classes. She didn't feel panicked like yesterday. She calmly observed everything and everyone. She looked around each classroom with extra care, thinking there might be a clue anywhere. There were lots of things that might have been important, but nothing that pointed to anyone specific.

At lunch, Becky sat alone, as usual. But today she only pretended to read. She surreptitiously glanced around the edge of her book and watched the other students.

Suddenly something bit her arm.

"Ouch!"

It felt like a mosquito or a fly. But when she looked, there was nothing there. She continued watching.

"Ouch!"

There it was again.

She looked over and saw some of the junior barbarians laughing. Brad had a big open-mouthed metal grin on his face.

She ignored them.

"Ouch!"

This time it was the top of her right ear. The junior barbarians laughed louder. But it couldn't have been them; she had been watching the whole time. Not one of them had even raised a finger, let alone thrown something.

The bell rang marking the end of lunch. Becky got up and walked to the library.

The calm of the library gave Becky a chance to go over everything she had seen and heard so far. She wheeled her cart-full of books through the stacks and thought carefully as she put them in their proper places on the shelves. There was the scratched paint by the office, and the mail slot. John Tyler had asked about bank fraud in Your Money and You. Maybe he was interested in a life of crime. The junior barbarians were on the warpath again, but that was nothing new. In English, Melissa Marek did a report on a book about tracking down computer hackers.

That was the most important detail. Becky'd had no idea Melissa was interested in computers. But even though Melissa wasn't very nice, Becky couldn't imagine her breaking into the school office.

Becky continued shelving the books from her cart. Perhaps Melissa and John were in it together. Hadn't John asked Melissa to the winter dance? Becky couldn't remember. Maybe John had broken into the office and Melissa'd changed the grade on the computer. But when? How did they get in when school was in session? It wasn't like when Ms. Alexander had let Becky in during vacation. Maybe John had a pet hamster that he trained to go in through the mail slot and unlock the door. Maybe he'd trained the hamster to change the grade!

Becky shook her head. What was she thinking? Ideas were stacking up all over the place inside her head. There wasn't room left to think clearly. She needed to form a good theory about what had happened. A hamster accessing the database wasn't it!

Becky didn't get much thinking done in Mr. O's class. The sub decided that it was time for a surprise quiz and really laid it on. Becky was surprised at how hard the test was. She figured the sub must have been getting back at the class for giving her such a hard time over the last few weeks.

When Becky got to the locker room for seventh period, she quickly changed into her gym clothes and filed out to the field with the rest of the girls. They lined up to wait for Coach Kimball.

"Oooh, what's in your hair, Becky?" Melissa Marek said. She and Jenny Sloat were standing next to her.

Becky tried to ignore her. She didn't need to be teased

today. Melissa reached her hand toward Becky's head. Becky took a step away.

"Chill out, Becky," Melissa sneered. "Look, there's really something here. I'm just trying to help."

She reached her hand up again and pulled something out of Becky's hair. She held it in front of Becky's face.

"Is this a new style?" Melissa said. "I don't think it will help." She and Jenny giggled.

Becky looked at Melissa's fingers. She held up a tiny bright green rubber band. Becky reached out and took it.

"Thanks," she mumbled.

"Gross!" said Jenny. "That's like the rubber bands my brother uses in his braces. And it was in her hair!"

"Maybe it's a new fashion statement," said another girl.

Coach Kimball's arrival stopped the girls' chattering. Becky stood looking at the ground, sliding the rubber band up and down her finger.

The coach was lecturing about the rules and strategy of soccer. Becky hated soccer. She wasn't listening anyway. She was focused on not getting upset. It was bad enough that she hadn't made any progress in finding the scum and the Kids were comming in only a few hours. She didn't need to be teased in P.E. as well.

*Just ignore them, Beck,* she said to herself. She recalled that in Alaska, Tlingit women used to put bear grease and feathers in their hair and the Tlingit men thought they were gorgeous. Jenny and Melissa didn't know anything about that.

Coach Kimball droned on in the background. Becky focused on her detective work. She pictured the school office. She had been at the computer three times in the last few weeks. Was there anything she noticed that could help? She pictured every desk, every chair. The floor and the walls. The windows. The principal's office. She thought about every move she'd made. Sneaking in through the copy room. Turning the computer on. Copying the database. Climbing back in through the window. Installing the spy-cam program. Connecting the cables. Fixing the power switch. Hiding the camera. Tying the cables in place. *Wait!*

Becky looked down at her hands. The rubber band was wrapped around her pinkie. Fixing the power switch . . . she had used a tiny rubber band just like this one, except it was bright red instead of bright green. But it was exactly the same. Fluorescent in color, and only a half-inch long. Becky had never seen a rubber band like this except for the one she'd found in the office.

Becky knew. She needed to be totally sure. But she *knew!*

"Yes!"

Coach Kimball looked at Becky.

"Are you sure, Becky? I'm surprised by your enthusiasm." She turned toward the other girls. "All right, Becky will be goalie for the B team."

Becky didn't even care. She actually smiled.

As soon as P.E. was over, Becky rushed to the lockers and changed. Then she ran to the main building. She ignored the fact that her arms and legs were aching from tending goal. She didn't stop to think how surprised and pleased she'd been when she'd blocked the winning goal. Or how her team, and Coach Kimball, had congratulated her. She didn't stop for anything. All that mattered was that she got there before *they* left.

In the main hall, students were swarming around lockers

and pushing through the crowds to get out of school for the weekend. Becky stood on tiptoe and peered up and down the hall. Halfway down she spotted who she was looking for. She casually walked along the side of the hall, trying not to be obvious. She stopped behind the drinking fountain and watched.

The junior barbarians were standing in a group against the opposite wall. Brad stood in the middle of them, smiling his steely smile. Becky waited. Suddenly a student stopped just in front of Brad and put his hand up to his neck—just like he'd been bitten by a mosquito. The student looked at Brad, who just smiled and shrugged. The student continued walking and the barbarians cracked up. A few moments later the same thing happened with another student.

Becky waited until the barbarians got bored and left. The halls were almost empty. She walked over to the spot where Brad had been standing. As she approached, she saw what she had been looking for: a half-dozen tiny green, red, and yellow rubber bands lay scattered on the floor.

# [17]

COMM TRANSCRIPT
COLLECTED BY CYBER.KDZ COMMBOT
TIME: 23:00 GMT (FRIDAY)
ONLINE:   TEREZA
          PAUL
          BECKY
          JOSH
          DEEDER
          SANJEEV
          LOREN
BEGIN TRANSCRIPT. . . . .

<Tereza>   Oi.
<Josh>     Hiya!
<Deeder>   Hallo
<Loren>    Hi.
<Sanjeev>  hey
<Paul>     Commander X sends greetings.
<Becky>    Hi, everyone. I've got big news!
<Tereza>   Go ahead, Becky.
<Becky>    I've got him! I figured out who the scum is!
<Deeder>   Him? The picture was of a girl . . .
<Becky>    I know. She's not the one who did it.
<Josh>     Then who?

```
<Becky>     Brad Sloat!
<Deeder>    Details. We need details.
<Becky>     Here's the shortest version I can give.
            Jenny Sloat is Brad's sister. She's got a
            crush on one of the guys on the football
            team. So to get him to notice her, she wants
            to be a cheerleader.
<Deeder>    Sounds like a typical American TV show.
<Becky>     Yeah, I know. But Jenny's parents said she
            couldn't be on the squad unless she
            improved her grades. The big problem is,
            she's failing history.
<Josh>      What's this got to do with your grade?
<Becky>     Hang on, Josh, I'll tell you. She can't
            fail, so she gets her big brother to change
            her grade for her.
<Deeder>    Why would he do that?
<Becky>     I'm not exactly sure, but I think he's
            making her do his jobs around the house or
            something. It doesn't matter. What does
            matter is that he changed her grade to an A.
<Deeder>    How did he get into the office?
<Becky>     I don't know. Brad gets into a lot of
            trouble. He's sent to the office for
            detention all the time. My guess is he was
            there after school one day and had a chance
            to do it.
<Tereza>    But what about your grade?
<Becky>     Brad doesn't like me.
<Tereza>    Why not?
<Becky>     I don't want to get into that right now.
            He's just a mean person. I think that while
            he was changing Jenny's grade, he thought
            it would be funny to change mine as well.
            That would be just like him.
<Josh>      What a jerk!
```

<Becky>    Yeah, he is. He's the leader of the junior barbarians.

<Sanjeev>  your school has a club called the junior barbarians?

<Becky>    No. That's just what I call these kids who enjoy being jerks.

<Deeder>   But how can you be sure this is what happened?

<Becky>    This part I am sure of. The power switch was broken on the back of the SpyCam when I set it up. I looked all over the place for something that was just the right size to keep the switch on. I found this tiny rubber band next to the computer. It was fluorescent red and really small. Just perfect for the switch. That rubber band came from Brad Sloat.

<Loren>    How can you be sure?

<Becky>    Yesterday at lunch I was shot with a rubber band, but I didn't know it at the time. Later, I found the rubber band in my hair. It was exactly like the one I used on the camera, except bright green. Jenny Sloat was there and said it was just like the rubber bands her brother used in his braces. That was the trigger that helped me figure this out. I went to watch Brad and the barbarians. They were standing in the hall picking on people. Brad was shooting rubber bands at kids when they walked by. But no one knew because he shoots them out of his mouth!

<Josh>     I had a friend in LA who could do that. He unhooks the band from his braces and lets it go with his tongue. He was a good shot, too.

| | |
|---|---|
| \<Becky\> | So is Brad. When I saw him doing that, I realized that he'd shot me at lunch. The rubber band got stuck in my hair. And the rubber band by the office computer proves that he did it. |
| \<Loren\> | But there are other people who wear braces at your school, yes? |
| \<Becky\> | Yeah. But no one's as mean as Brad. |
| \<Josh\> | I think Becky's right. All the pieces fit. |
| \<Deeder\> | Wow. It does sound pretty good. |
| \<Becky\> | Thanks. |
| \<Tereza\> | I think Becky is right as well. But we should be sure. This is a lot of circumstantial evidence. |
| \<Paul\> | What's circumstantial? |
| \<Tereza\> | It means we have lots of facts that say Brad did it but we don't have proof, like a photo or a fingerprint. |
| \<Paul\> | He's a big jerk. Isn't that proof enough? |
| \<Tereza\> | I don't think so. |
| \<Sanjeev\> | i think paulie's got a point. just nail him. |
| \<Loren\> | No. We should make sure. And now that we have all this evidence, it will be very easy. |
| \<Becky\> | How, Loren? |
| \<Loren\> | Since we have a suspect, we must get him to confess. |
| \<Becky\> | That will be hard. He'll just lie. He's good at that. |
| \<Loren\> | But there is someone involved that probably is not so good at lying. |
| \<Paul\> | Jenny? |
| \<Loren\> | Oui! I think we can figure out a way to use Jenny to trap Brad. |
| \<Josh\> | How? |

```
<Loren>      I'm not sure yet. Sanj, how far have you
             progressed with Paul's game?
<Paul>       It better be a lot cause I'm getting tired
             of this curry stuff.
<Sanjeev>    i've got the basics nailed. should have a
             working beta in a few days.
<Loren>      Becky, did you and Paul receive two
             cameras?
<Becky>      Yeah. I used one for the spy-cam, and the
             other is still hooked to our computer.
<Deeder>     Wheels are turning in that head, huh,
             Loren?
<Loren>      We will see. Becky, you and I will comm
             tomorrow. I think we can figure something
             out. We will let everyone know what we come
             up with.
<Becky>      OK.
<Deeder>     I have one more question.
<Becky>      Yeah?
<Deeder>     If Brad's the scum who changed the grades,
             who's the girl the spy-cam caught?
<Becky>      I'll tell you later.
<Deeder>     How come?
<Becky>      Just drop it for now, Deeder. I promise
             I'll tell you.
<Tereza>     I think we should cut this short before you
             two start arguing. Everyone check for
             Loren's emails. Adeus.
<Becky>      So long. Thanks everyone!
<Paul>       Commander X signing off.
<Sanjeev>    bye
<Josh>       Take care.
<Loren>      bye.
<Deeder>     Daag
[TEREZA HAS LOGGED OFF]
[BECKY HAS LOGGED OFF]
```

```
[PAUL HAS LOGGED OFF]
[SANJEEV HAS LOGGED OFF]
[JOSH HAS LOGGED OFF]
[LOREN HAS LOGGED OFF]
[DEEDER HAS LOGGED OFF]
COMM TRANSCRIPT COMPLETE
CYBER.KDZ COMMBOT TERMINATING EXECUTION
TIME: 23:10 GMT
```

# [18]

It had been a week since the last Cyber.kdz comm. Becky and Loren had commed for hours over the weekend. They had thought of a dozen strategies. Loren wanted to execute the plan remotely and anonymously, but Becky insisted—without explaining why—that she have an active role. Finally, they agreed on a course of action. Many more emails had been exchanged on Monday. Deeder did some Internet research on Tuesday and then helped Sanj with the programming. They were finished by Thursday and the plan was set for Friday. Today was Friday.

Becky checked her watch as she rolled her cart of books between the stacks.

*Should be about now* . . . she said to herself, and turned the cart down the aisle that led toward the computer lab.

The Bennington-Carver computer lab occupied a separate section of the library that extended off the main reading area. It wasn't separated by a wall like the audio-visual room. Instead, one entire side was open to the rest of the library. The quiet clacking of keys could be heard throughout.

Becky wheeled the cart to the end of the 200 row. She didn't have any books to shelve here, but it was the closest row to the lab. She could look through the shelf and see perfectly.

Jenny Sloat sat down at the workstation next to Melissa. Her friend was already working. Jenny arranged her chair, tilted the monitor up and down, and set her papers in a neat pile next to the keyboard. Finally she looked down at her assignment sheet:

*Virtual Field Trip to Malaysia*
*You must visit as many World Wide Web sites as possible that relate to the country of Malaysia. Create a report of what you find. Include the following facts in your report . . .*

"Oh, boring," Jenny said under her breath. "Like, why couldn't I get to visit Dallas or San Francisco . . . somewhere with a football team with real cheerleaders . . ."

Slowly she followed the directions printed on her assignment. She entered the address for the Yahoo search engine and then entered "Malaysia" in the search field. Yahoo spit back the results of her search. She selected *The Official Page of the Malaysian Tourism Board*. The screen went blank for a moment as the browser began loading the data from the site. Then the page appeared.

## COMPUTER CRIME NOTIFICATION
## SECURITY CHECK

The following is intended for viewing by

☞ <u>JENNY SLOAT</u> ☜

By clicking on your name above, you acknowledge that
you are the named party and agree to be bound by the
rules and regulations of the Internet Patrol.

Jenny blinked. She had clicked on *The Malaysia Tourism Page* and was supposed to be looking at a map of Malaysia. She retyped the address, but the same message appeared. She clicked the "reload" button. The message stayed the same. Jenny looked around. Becky ducked and tried to look busy. Everyone else was busy at their terminals. It was clear that Jenny wasn't sure what she should do. Finally, she shrugged and clicked on her name. A new page appeared.

## COMPUTER CRIME NOTIFICATION
## FROM: INTERNET PATROL
## TO: JENNY SLOAT

☞ <u>Message Follows</u> ☜

Our office has learned that you have been involved in a
serious database-tampering crime. We have received infor-

mation that there is an international ring of saboteurs altering and destroying sensitive data at various government and educational institutions. Recent actions on your part point to your participation in this illegal organization.

The Internet Patrol assumes innocence before guilt. Therefore, we are sending this warning to you. If the tampering of the database was inadvertent or caused by a temporary lack of judgment, you now have the opportunity to correct the problem. If all database changes are reversed by 7 P.M. this evening, we will cancel our investigation.

You should be reminded that if the database changes are not reversed and you are found guilty, the results of our investigation will be supplied to the school principal as well as the United States Cheerleading Society, who may take the serious action of banning you from all squad participation for the rest of your life.

You choose.

Sincerely,
The Internet Patrol


P.S. You can tell Brad that he will most likely go to jail.

Melissa leaned over from her workstation.

"Hey, Jenny, what are you looking at?" she whispered.

Jenny quickly clicked off the computer.

"Oh, nothing," she answered hurriedly. "I think my computer's broken."

"You should get on a different workstation, then. We only have twenty minutes to finish our assignment. Hey, are you okay?"

Jenny looked kind of pale.

"I don't know. I'm feeling a little sick. Maybe I should go to the nurse . . ."

She walked over to Ms. Lee, the computer lab teacher. When Ms. Lee saw how pale Jenny looked and how sweaty her brow was, she gave her permission to go to the nurse immediately.

Becky grabbed three books off her cart, told the librarian she had to deliver them to Ms. Alexander's class and carefully followed Jenny out of the library.

Once in the hall, Jenny ran to the 300 building. She stood on tiptoe and looked into one of the classrooms. Becky watched from around the corner as Jenny frantically waved through the window. A few minutes later, Brad was in the hall, whispering angrily.

*"What are you doing?"* he said. *"What's the matter? Do you know how embarrassing it is to have to ask to go to the bathroom in the middle of class so I can come out here?"*

Jenny didn't bother answering.

"Brad, we have a big problem." She told him about the message from the Internet Patrol.

"That's so stupid," Brad scoffed. "There's no Internet Patrol."

"How do you know? If there isn't one, then how did they find out what we did? I'm really scared. I may never get to be a cheerleader. *Ever!*"

"Who cares about stupid cheerleading?"

"And, like, *you* might go to jail."

"*What!* What are you *talking* about?"

"I forgot to tell you that part. It said, *'You can tell Brad that he will most likely go to jail.'*"

"They knew *my* name too?" There was worry in his voice.

"That's what it said."

Brad shook his head, trying to rid himself of the doubt he felt.

"This is dumb. This is some lame computer joke. I'm not letting a stupid hacker make a fool of me." He turned to go back to his class.

Jenny grabbed his arm.

"Brad! You can't go!" she pleaded. "You've gotta help me. I can't change the database by myself. At least tell me what to do."

Brad turned angrily toward her.

"You're not changing anything. You're so dumb you'll screw it up . . . or get caught . . ."

"I *am* changing it," Jenny challenged. "With you or without you. I don't care if you think this is a joke. I'm not taking a chance on getting banned from cheerleading for life."

"You moron! They can't do that."

"How do you know?" Jenny asked. She was really upset now. "I don't wanna find out. I'm changing the grades back."

"I'm telling you, you'll get caught. Then you'll be in more trouble," Brad said, trying to scare her.

"I don't care," Jenny replied and then added. "And if I get caught, I'll tell them *you* changed the grades first."

"You fink, Jenny!"

Jenny just stood and glowered at her brother.

"They won't believe you . . ."

Jenny continued to stare.

"They'll need proof . . ."

Jenny didn't say a word.

147

Brad saw that Jenny wasn't changing her mind. He knew he had to help her to protect himself.

"All right," he said, "I don't know what I did to get a sister like you."

"Guess you were just lucky," she said, grinning.

"Yeah, sure," Brad replied. "Listen, I'll do something to get put on detention today. You call Mom and tell her we'll be home late."

"She'll ask why . . ."

"Make something up. Do I have to do everything? Tell her we're trying out for the school play. Come to the office at four-thirty. Tell the secretary you're picking me up. I'll take care of the rest. And don't tell anyone else about this—got it?"

"Yeah, I got it. I'm not stupid," Jenny snapped.

"Could've fooled me. What do I get this time?"

Jenny stared. "What are you talking about? This is to save *your* butt as well as mine. Besides, I'm already doing all your chores and giving you my allowance for three months."

Their discussion was cut short by the bell marking the end of fifth period. The classroom doors swung open and students began pouring into the halls.

"We'll agree on something later," Brad said, and turned to go to his next class.

Becky watched the two head down the hall. She smiled to herself and then turned back toward the library.

It was 4:30. Jenny pushed through the doors and into the school office. The woman behind the counter smiled.

"Can I help you?"

Jenny smiled back. "Yes, please. I'm here to pick up my brother, Brad Sloat. He's on detention, I think."

The woman stopped smiling. "When is he ever *not* on detention?" she asked, not expecting an answer. She stuck her thumb toward the teachers' staff room. "He's in there. I don't know why these teachers can't keep kids like him in their own classrooms."

"Thank you," Jenny said, with her prettiest smile. She turned and went through the door the woman had indicated. She passed through the copy room and into the staff room. The room was empty except for one teacher rearranging things in the refrigerator, and Brad, who was sitting at the table, staring at his shoes.

"Can you go home now, Brad?" Jenny said in falsely sweet voice.

"Not yet. I have a few more minutes."

The teacher at the fridge turned and said, "You can go. It's close enough."

Brad smiled. "No way. If it got back to Ms. Kalonick that I didn't stay for my full detention, she'd be really mad. I'll stay."

Jenny sat down next to her brother. They didn't say anything. After another minute, the teacher shut the fridge, gathered his things, and left the room.

"Finally!" Brad said, as he grabbed Jenny's hand. "Hurry, before someone else comes!"

He pulled her behind him toward one of the doors leading off the staff room.

"In here, quick," he said, and pushed her in front of him.

They were in a very dark closet. Jenny couldn't see anything. She felt Brad lean close.

"I hope you went to the bathroom already, 'cause we've got a long wait."

\*     \*     \*

The tiny light from Brad's watch reflected off his braces. He looked up at Jenny.

"Six-forty-five. It's time," he whispered. "Don't say anything and don't touch anything. Understand?"

"Yes." Right now Jenny would agree to anything if it meant getting out of that smelly closet and stretching her legs.

Brad opened the door and they crept out slowly. The overhead fluorescents were off. The early evening light through the windows made everything drab and gray. Jenny followed Brad through the copy room to the office. He sat down at the computer. She stood next to him.

He reached around and flipped on the power switch.

"What's taking so long?" Jenny whispered.

"This computer is slow," Brad said. "Just hold on."

When the computer booted up, Brad opened the grades database.

"Are you sure you want to do this? It's probably the only A you'll ever get," Brad taunted.

"Look who's talking," Jenny said. "If you hadn't changed *your* grades, you wouldn't have even had a D average this semester."

Jenny watched as Brad changed her wonderful A in history to an F. Then he changed the B she'd given herself in English to a D. Then he brought up his grades and replaced the line of B's with C's, D's, and F's.

"That's it. Let's get out of here." Brad reached around to turn off the computer.

"Wait! What about Becky's history grade?"

"Forget that. In fact, while we're here, why don't we change the rest of that brainiac's grades to F's . . . ?" Brad pulled up Becky's records.

"I wouldn't do that if I were you."

Brad jumped. Jenny screamed.

"What the . . . ?" Brad exclaimed.

A tiny image stepped into the middle of the computer screen. It was kind of like a cartoon, but not exactly—a little like a real person on a TV screen, but not quite. It wore a baseball cap with the initials "IP" on it. The brim was pulled down so you couldn't make out its face. It spoke again, its voice sounding tinny through the little speaker inside the computer.

"I wouldn't do that," it said.

*"The Internet Patrol . . ."* Jenny whispered.

"It is not," said Brad. "It's some stupid computer game, or something."

Brad used the mouse to highlight Becky's geometry grade.

The little character pushed the mouse pointer off the grade.

Brad moved it over again.

The character pushed the highlight away a second time.

Jenny giggled.

"It's kind of cute . . ."

"Stuff it," Brad snapped. He was getting angry. "Some stupid program's not gonna stop me from changing her grades . . ."

Brad tried to change one of the other grades, but the little character kept moving the mouse pointer around the screen.

*"You stupid thing!"* Brad yelled in frustration.

The little character stopped and turned to face Brad. It lifted its arms and then zoomed right off the top of the screen.

"Where'd it go?" asked Jenny.

*THUMP!*

Something landed loudly behind them.

Brad and Jenny spun around. A figure stood in the dim light. It wore a baseball cap with the brim pulled down to hide its face.

Jenny dug her nails into Brad's shoulder as she backed away, her eyes big as saucers. Brad sat frozen in his chair.

The figure reached up and removed the cap. Becky shook her hair out and stood smiling.

"Becky?" Jenny gasped.

Brad's expression changed from fright to anger. Jenny still stood wide-eyed.

"Better change my grade back, Brad, since you were the one who messed it up in the first place."

Recovering himself, Brad stared at Becky belligerently.

"Says you. You can't prove *anything*."

Becky smiled. "Oh, yeah?"

She took a few steps, reached around Brad, and pressed a couple of keys. A window opened in the bottom corner of the screen. In it was the feed from the video camera. Becky punched a few more keys. The live shot was replaced with a few seconds of video replay. Jenny and Brad stared open mouthed as they watched the tiny image of the two of them in front of the computer just a few moments before. The audio from the speaker wasn't very good, but they could understand the conversation.

*"Are you sure you want to do this? It's probably the only A you'll ever get."*

*"Look who's talking. If you hadn't changed your grades, you wouldn't have even had a D average this semester."*

The nine-second clip repeated itself over and over.

Brad scowled. "How did you get that?"

Becky was loving this. She tried not to laugh in Brad's

face. She walked around the computer to the philodendron and slowly pushed a few leaves aside, exposing the camera.

Jenny took a breath. "Wow," she said, her eyes big. "You're in the Internet Patrol, aren't you?"

"Shut up, you idiot!" Brad said. "She's not in anything. This was a set-up."

"Better fix my grade soon," Becky said, motioning toward the clock on the wall. "You only have four minutes until seven o'clock."

Jenny looked up at the clock. "Hurry, Brad. Do it!"

"She's making this up, Jenny," Brad said, irritation evident in his voice. "That whole thing about the Internet Patrol was a big lie to trick us."

Becky smiled again. "Might be. But do you want to take that chance?"

Brad looked at Becky, then at Jenny, then at the clock. He was mad. But he was trapped.

Quickly he pounded the keys and replaced Becky's F with an A+. Then he exited the grades database.

"Smart choice," Becky said. She reached into the philodendron and casually removed the rubber band holding the power switch on. The switch clicked off.

Instantly the video disappeared from the screen. A new screen appeared. Jenny and Brad leaned forward to read it.

```
::::::::::::::::::::::::::::::::::::::::::::::::::::::::::::::::::::::::::::::::::
```

## COMPUTER CRIME NOTIFICATION
## FROM: INTERNET PATROL
## TO: JENNY SLOAT, BRAD SLOAT

☞ Message Follows ☜

Our office would like to congratulate you on your wise deci-
sion. Our investigation will be suspended and no further action will be taken against you.

However, and this is a big however, we will archive our
computer and video records and they will be transferred immediately to the appropriate authorities if any of the following occurs:
  1. We receive a report that you are involved in computer
     espionage of any sort.
  2. We receive directions from Agent Becky Strahn to do so.
Thus, we suggest that you clean up your act.
Understand?

Sincerely,
The Internet Patrol

P.S. We'll be watching . . .

```
::::::::::::::::::::::::::::::::::::::::::::::::::::::::::::::::::::::::::::::::::
```

"See, Brad?" Jenny whispered, "I told you she was
with the Internet Patrol . . ."

Brad didn't reply. He got up slowly and walked over
to Becky. He stood close, real close, and glared at her.
He was a good head taller than she was. His hands were

rolled into fists and his teeth were clenched. He wanted to scare her . . . scare her bad.

But Becky didn't move.

They stared at each other for a full minute. Becky knew that Brad was waiting for her to show some sign of fear. She knew he was angry because she'd nailed him. She knew he wanted her to back down.

But Becky didn't back down. She looked him right in the eye and didn't move a muscle. Finally she spoke.

"You don't scare me, Brad. I don't care if you like me or hate me or if you get a whole *troop* of barbarians following you that hate me, too. You might think I'm this lonely girl you can pick on. But you can't. Because nothing you do is gonna change the fact that I have plenty of friends—all over the world. And they know who I am and what I'm worth, and they're on my side. So next time we pass in the hall, before you shove me, or knock my books out of my arms, or call me names, remember that *we're smarter than you are.* And we look after each other. And you can't stop us."

In the dim light Becky thought she could see Brad turn several shades of red. His face was all tight as he tried to think of something to say. But he couldn't. Finally he spun around, grabbed Jenny's arm, and said, "C'mon, let's go."

"Oh, Brad. There's one more thing . . ."

Brad stopped halfway to the door and turned toward Becky.

"You forgot this."

Becky raised her hand, took careful aim, and then nailed Brad right between the eyes with a tiny fluorescent red rubber band.

# [19]

From: **Becky**, historian@nyc.net.us
To: **Cyber.kdz**, thekids@cyber.kdz.net
Date: Fri, 21:31 (Sat, 02:31 GMT)
Subject: The Story Ends

Hey Kids,
It's over. And it was perfect! Couldn't have gone better. I
have all of you to thank for that. What great friends you
are!

Jenny really freaked when the Internet Patrol message appeared. She asked the teacher if she could go to the nurse,
so I followed her. She got Brad out of class and told him
what happened. He didn't care at first, but Jenny convinced
him to change the grades back. So all I had to do was wait
for them. The problem was getting into the office. Luckily,
Steph, the woman who works on the computer, thinks I'm a
total computer genius. Right before she left for the day, I told
her there might be a virus on her machine. So she left me
there to take a look. I installed the new programs Deeder and
Sanj wrote and then waited until almost everyone was out of
the office. When no one was looking I hid under a desk until
they locked up the school. Then I set up the second camera

behind a file cabinet where I could stay out of sight but still see what was going on.

Brad and Jenny showed up right on time. I captured a great video clip of them at the computer. And using the Air Destruction code was a great idea! It really freaked them out. Jenny almost had a heart attack when I jumped out from my hiding place. It actually seemed like I flew right out of the computer and landed behind them. Brad was like a trapped rat. He couldn't figure out how everything could go so wrong. He finally gave in and changed the grades. But then tried his bully tactics on me. I gave him a lecture and a friendly parting shot as well. I think the junior barbarians won't bug me . . . at least for a while.

I packed up the cameras, erased the programs, and made sure everything was just like it was before this whole thing started. Boy, was it nice to get out of the office! It was beginning to feel like I spent more time there than at home.

Every one of you has been so great. I never would have thought someone had changed my grade if not for Loren. And if it wasn't for Deeder's stubborn (I mean that in a nice way, Deed!) insistence that we go after the scum, I wouldn't have found out who did it. If Paul hadn't eaten all that curry, Sanj would never have started the Air Destruction code. All your support made it happen. Thank you. You're the best. And that makes it harder to say what I have to say.

During the last few months I started to forget who I was. I let some jerks who didn't know me affect what I thought of myself. I forgot that I'm a pretty neat person and that that's why you're my friends. Instead, I thought of myself as an ugly person. A person no one likes. A fat person. And because of that, I did something I'm really ashamed of. I lied to my best friends: the Kids. That picture in the yearbook isn't me; it's my friend Kim. I'm really the girl that the spy-cam caught. I'm not the gorgeous blond. I'm the plain old me.

There have been so many people during the last year who didn't care about who I was. They only cared about what I looked like. I was scared that Cyber.kdz would think that way, too. But now I remember who I am. And that's what matters the most. I'd be really sorry if any of you didn't like me because of the way I look. I'd be really sad. But it won't change what I think of myself.

I'm sorry I lied to you. I hope you can forgive me.

Becky

P.S. Loren, I put some real pictures of me on CKServer if you want to get rid of the pictures of Kim. That is, if you still want me in the yearbook.

---

From: **Tereza**, tereza.ctmc@macnet.com.br
To: **Becky**, historian@nyc.net.us
Date: Sat, 08:09 (Sat, 11:09 GMT)
Subject: Re: The Story Ends

Querida amiga,

I am sure it was very hard for you to send the email. Cyber.kdz is your home and we are your family. Don't forget it.

Quando seu coração esta cheio de amor
Sua face transparece em beleza.

That means:
When your heart is full
Beauty is in your face.

Don't forget.

Com todo o meu coração,

*73*

---

From: **Sanjeev**, sanj!metalman@music.indiaU.edu.in
To: **Becky**, historian@nyc.net.us
Date: Sat, 18:35 (Sat, 12:35 GMT)
Subject: Re: The Story Ends

glad you got your head screwed back on straight. don't
know what you were thinking. like you just the way you are.
don't change. just eat curry.

---

From: **Loren**, loren.jouet@sun.com.fr
To: **Becky**, historian@nyc.net.us
Date: Sat, 16:52 (Sat, 15:52 GMT)
Subject: Re: The Story Ends

Mon Ami,

The moment I read your message I added the real pictures to
the yearbook. That is where you belong.

Ton ami,

L

From: **Josh**, joshthealien@aol.com
To: **Becky**, historian@nyc.net.us
Date: Sat, 08:03 (Sat, 16:03 GMT)
Subject: Re: The Story Ends

Dear Becky,

I'm not the only one who does crazy things sometimes, huh? I know what it's like to forget how great Cyber.kdz is. Glad you remembered. Welcome back.

Love,
Josh

---

From: **Paul**, commx@nyc.net.us
To: **Becky**, historian@nyc.net.us
Date: Sat, 15:47 (Sat, 20:47 GMT)
Subject: Re: The Story Ends

Told you so.

Commander X

P.S. Since you used the Air Destruction code, *you* have to finish the rest of the curry!

---

From: **Deeder**, rodan@netherspace.nl
To: **Becky**, historian@nyc.net.us
Date: Sat, 22:45 (Sat, 21:45 GMT)
Subject: Re: The Story Ends

Beck-Babe,

I don't care what you look like. I'm glad you're straight with us now. Guess that makes us even after what I pulled a while back when I ignored the Cyber.kdz vote. We all make mistakes.

I only have one question. I took a look at the "real" pictures of you that Loren put in the yearbook. What's the matter with your hair?

Your friend in crime,
Deed

---

From: **Becky**, historian@nyc.net.us
To: **Deeder**, rodan@netherspace.nl
Date: Sat, 18:17 (Sat, 23:17 GMT)
Subject: Attack

Deer Deeder,
I can't believe you would say something so cruel after what I've just been through. I told you I'm really insecure about all this and the first thing you do is criticize my looks. Some friend you are.

To answer your question, that is not my hair.

I'm being attacked by a mop.

Love,
Becky

# AUTHOR'S NOTE

I used a lot of software and hardware to research, write, and edit this book. I thought you might be interested in what I've chosen. Here's the list:

Word for Windows 6.0a
Excel 4.0
WinFax Pro 4.0d
Pegasus Mail for Windows 2.23
Netscape Navigator 2.0
Trumpet Winsock 2.1f
WinCim 1.4
A Zillion Kajillion Rhymes 2.01

Dell Dimension XPS P90 Pentium
    (1 GB Hard Drive, 16 MB RAM,
    Triple-Speed CD-ROM #9 GXE Video)
ViewSonic 17G 17'' monitor
Practical Peripherals PM 288MT II V.34 Modem
Altima 486 SLC Greyscale Notebook
    (120MB Hard Drive, 4 MB RAM)
HP Laser Jet Series II Printer

Some of this stuff's pretty old, I know. But I'm so busy writing that it's hard to upgrade *every* piece of software. I got rid of the old Compaq portable I used on *Cyber.kdz #1* and rented the

Altima 486 Notebook. I needed it because I was traveling in Greece for a while.

Don't waste your time trying to find the Kids' yearbook on the Web. The security is very tight and the URL isn't published. Even if you did find CKServer (which you won't), you couldn't get in. But there is a lot of cool stuff to take a look at on the Web—start with http://cyber.kdz.com! Just remember to surf sensibly and *never* give out your name or phone number without your parents' permission.

Be good.

157

# Glossary of Cyber.kdz Slang
## and Other Words You Might Want to Know

**501:** Excuse that's full of holes.

**BEAM:** Real-time chat line that is private to the Kids.

**BROWSER:** Software used to surf the Web. Thread sled.

**BROWSING:** To follow links from page to page on the World Wide Web.

**CANCER:** Deadly virus.

**COMM AND COMMING:** To communicate via email or real-time text messages.

**COMMBOT:** Program that automatically logs the conversation during a Cyber.kdz comm.

**DRIVEL:** 99% of what passes through the net.

**FAILS:** Stinks.

**FLAME:** A mean or angry message.

**FLU:** Bad virus.

**FRISBEE:** CD-ROM

**FRY A SCREEN:** Send a flame.

**FTP:** Method for transferring files across the Internet.

**GMT:** Greenwich Mean Time: the time at the Prime Meridian (0° longitude), which runs through Greenwich, England (just outside of London). Time zones are often described in relation to GMT. For example, Pacific Standard Time (PST) on the West Coast of the United States is eight hours (-0800) behind GMT. Also known as UTC (Universal Coordinated Time).

**GODZILLA:** Computer owned by Deeder that is tricked out and optimized for detecting and destroying flus and cancers.

**GREPPER or GREPHEAD:** Someone who is really into UNIX. (Comes from the UNIX command *grep*.).

**JAVA:** Programming language for writing programs that can be run on the World Wide Web. The programs are called "applets."

**KID:** Fellow member of Cyber.kdz.

**LINKS:** A connection between pages on the WWW. Links allow you to quickly jump between different Web sites.

**NET:** The Internet.

**PAGES:** Documents on the Web. Pages can contain text, graphics, sound, animation, and video.

**PERCOLATOR:** Program for the Web written in JAVA (an applet).

**SCUM OF THE EARTH:** People who create cancers.

**SLIDE THE TALKWAYS:** Surf the Net.

**SPIN THE WEB:** Surf.

**STIKS:** Shirt, Tie, Keyboard. Boring corporate computer people.

**TALKWAY:** The Wire.

**THE WIRE:** The Internet.

**THREAD SLED:** World Wide Web Browser. Software used to spin the web.

**WEB:** World Wide Web.

**WORLD WIDE WEB:** Often referred to as "The Web." A collection of servers all over the world which provide *pages* of text, graphics, sound, and video. There are Web pages dealing with every subject from selling soft drinks to writing children's books. Pages can be connected to other pages with *links*. Clicking on a link brings you to the linked page. Since nearly every page on the Web has links to other pages, you can spend a great deal of time *browsing* pages—jumping from one to another to another to another.

**WWW:** See World Wide Web.

# Foreign Language Terms

| | |
|---|---|
| **Adeus** | Portuguese: Goodbye |
| **Até mais** | Portuguese: Until then |
| **Au revoir** | French: Goodbye |
| **Beijos** | Portuguese: Kisses |
| **Boa noite** | Portuguese: Good evening; good night |
| **Bon appétit** | French: Good appetite; enjoy your meal |
| **Bonsoir** | French: Good evening |
| **C'est bon** | French: This is good |
| **C'est incroyable** | French: It is incredible |
| **C'est vrai** | French: This is true |
| **Claro** | Portuguese: Of course |
| **Com todo o meu coração** | Portuguese: With all my heart |
| **Daag** | Dutch: Goodbye |
| **Et moi** | French: And me |
| **Fantastique** | French: Fantastic |
| **Félicitations** | French: Congratulations |
| **Gaaf** | Dutch: Cool |
| **Hallo** | Dutch: Hello |
| **Hallo** | French: Hello |
| **Ja** | Dutch: Yes |
| **Je suis d'accord** | French: I agree |
| **Kemcho** | Indian: Hello |
| **Merci** | French: Thank you |
| **Merci beaucoup** | French: Thank you very much |
| **Mes meilleurs amis** | French: My best friends |
| **Meu querido** | Portuguese: My dear |
| **Mon ami** | French: My friend |
| **Oi** | Portuguese: Hello |
| **Oui** | French: Yes |

| | |
|---|---|
| **Oujo** | Indian: Goodbye |
| **Querida amiga** | Portuguese: Dear friend |
| **Queridos amigos** | Portuguese: Dear friends |
| **S'il vous plaît** | French: Please |
| **Senhor** | Portuguese: Mr. |
| **Sinceramente** | Portuguese: Sincerely |
| **Sr.** | Portuguese: Senhor; Mr. |
| **Sua amiga** | Portuguese: Your friend |
| **Ton ami** | French: Your friend |
| **Très chic** | French: Very chic; very fashionable |
| **Um beijo** | Portuguese: A kiss |

# Surf the Sites the Kids surf:

MALAYSIA'S HOMEPAGE
http://www.jaring.my/

*One of Becky's favorite sites:*
ARCHAEOLOGY AND ARCHITECTURE
http://www.xs4all.nl/~mkosian/

*One of Sanjeev's favorite sites:*
CyberINDIA™ Recipes and Food
http://www.cyberindia.net/cyberindia/links/i1recipe.htm

*One of Paul's favorite sites:*
VIRTUAL REALITY VIRTUAL REALITY RESOURCE LINKS
http://www.autonomy.com/virtual.htm

*Some of Loren's favorite sites:*
YAHOO'S LIST OF ELEVATOR COMPANIES
http://www.yahoo.com/business__and__economy/companies/
Industrial__Supplies/Materials__Handling/Conveyor__Systems/
Elevators/

*and, of course . . .*
BRUCE BALAN'S OFFICE
http://www.wenet.net/~balan

*and*
THE CYBER.KDZ WEB SITE
http://cyber.kdz.com

*Sorry—CKServer, the Cyber.kdz server, is off-limits. You can't go there!*

Stay tuned for more exciting
cyber-adventures as the Kids
try to save NASA
from a vicious virus in
**Cyber.kdz #3:**
**The Great NASA Flu**
coming from Avon Camelot
in July 1997.

# From out of the Shadows…
## Stories Filled with Mystery and Suspense by
# MARY DOWNING HAHN

### TIME FOR ANDREW
72469-3/$4.50 US/$5.99 Can

### DAPHNE'S BOOK
72355-7/$4.50 US/$6.50 Can

### THE TIME OF THE WITCH
71116-8/ $3.99 US/ $4.99 Can

### STEPPING ON THE CRACKS
71900-2/ $4.50 US/ $5.99 Can

### THE DEAD MAN IN INDIAN CREEK
71362-4/ $4.50 US/ $5.99 Can

### THE DOLL IN THE GARDEN
70865-5/ $4.50 US/ $5.99 Can

### FOLLOWING THE MYSTERY MAN
70677-6/ $4.50 US/ $5.99 Can

### TALLAHASSEE HIGGINS
70500-1/ $4.50 US/ $5.99 Can

### WAIT TILL HELEN COMES
70442-0/·$4.50 US/ $5.99 Can

### THE SPANISH KIDNAPPING DISASTER
71712-3/ $3.99 US/ $4.99 Can

### THE JELLYFISH SEASON
71635-6/ $3.99 US/ $5.50 Can

### THE SARA SUMMER
72354-9/ $4.50 US/ $5.99 Can

# IF YOU DARE TO BE SCARED...
# READ SPINETINGLERS!
## by M.T. COFFIN